P9-DIJ-265

This is a work of fiction. Any references to historical events, real people, or real places are used fictitiously. Other names, characters, places, and events are products of the author's imagination, and any resemblance to actual events or places or persons, living or dead, is entirely coincidental.

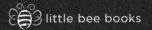 little bee books

New York, New York
Copyright © 2019 by Little Bee Books
All rights reserved, including the right of reproduction in whole
or in part in any form.
Manufactured in China   RRD 0321
First Edition 10 9 8 7 6 5 4 3 2
ISBN 978-1-4998-0998-5
littlebeebooks.com

For information about special discounts on bulk purchases, please
contact Little Bee Books at sales@littlebeebooks.com.

ELLA AND OWEN

4 BOOKS IN 1!

#1
THE CAVE OF
AAAAAH! DOOM!

#2
ATTACK OF THE
STINKY FISH MONSTER!

#3
KNIGHTS VS. DRAGONS

#4
THE EVIL
PUMPKIN PIE FIGHT

by Jaden Kent

illustrated by Iryna Bodnaruk

little bee books

BOOK 1

ELLA AND OWEN

THE CAVE OF AAAAAH! DOOM!

by Jaden Kent

illustrated by Iryna Bodnaruk

TABLE OF CONTENTS

On the other side of Fright Mountain, through the Fog of Screams and past the Waterfall of Destruction, was a place where only knights in shining armor dared to go when they wanted to impress a princess.

At the bottom of the other side of the
mountain was Dragon Patch. Dozens of
dragons lived there in dozens of stone
houses.

That's right.

Dragons!

Do you know all there is to know about dragons? Here are a few important things:

They have really stinky breath—actually, really stinky *fire* breath.

You can ride them like a flying horse!

They have wings.

And claws.

And their favorite dessert is pickled-fish Popsicles!
Is there more?
You bet! They sometimes get sick. And when fire-breathing dragons sneeze, you had better run for cover. . . .

"AH-CHOO!"

A ball of fire shot from Owen's mouth. It shot across his bedroom, out the window, and then lit on fire a toadstool that his twin sister, Ella, was sitting on.

"Blazing scales! You made me drop my spider snail!" Ella said as her eight-legged pet slimed away. Very slowly.

"Sorry," Owen said.

"You've been sick since forever," Ella said. "At least five whole days. And fire sneezes are *not* normal."

"But I'm okay being sick," Owen said.

Owen may have been okay being sick, but there was a long list of things Owen *wasn't* okay with. The top three were:

1. Evil Wizards

2. Vegetables
YUCK!
SCARY!

3. Evil Wizards Made of Vegetables
THE WORST!

Owen was very okay having a cold because it meant he could stay in bed and read. All day. Owen *loved* to read about hairy trolls, magical fairies, and heroic dragons. He especially loved books about dragons who defeated knights in shining armor.

"Mom says if I keep the slugs out of my ears and eat my slime, I'll be flying around in no time," Owen explained as he lifted a large rock and slurped the green gunk on the bottom. Owen's nose wiggled. He was going to sneeze again. *"Ah...ah...ah..."*

Ella flew into Owen's bedroom cave and grabbed a bucket of cold swamp water that was sitting by his bed. She threw it into his open mouth before he could sneeze flames. Steam puffed from his ears.

"There! That should do it!" Ella said.

Owen quickly shook his head. *"AH-CHOO!"* he sneezed.

A spray of water shot from his mouth and soaked Ella.

"*Yuck!* Sick brother!" Ella shook like a wet pixie at Lava Lake.

"Mom says I'll be fine in, like, a day or two . . . or ten." Owen turned away from his sister, cracked open a very good book about a dragon who defeated an evil wizard made of vegetables, and began to read it.

"*I* don't want you to be sick anymore," Ella said.

"Aww . . . thanks for caring, Sis!" Owen said.

"Well, it's kinda mostly because I know Mom will make me do your chores if you're sick," Ella admitted.

Owen looked straight ahead and ignored his sister.

She tried to get his attention again. "So, I've heard of a cave where a mystical wizard dragon has a secret cure for everything. He once changed a frog into a toad. He even turned a potato into something called a French fry—or so I'm told."

"Sorry, I don't want to go," Owen said and went back to reading his book.

"But it'll be an awesome adventure!" Ella said.

"Now for *sure* I don't want to go," he said.

"And exciting!" Ella added.

"I double even *more* don't want to go."
He turned a page in his book. The evil
wizard made of vegetables had just cast a
broccoli spell.

"*And* we can collect
ogre toenails for your
ogre toenail collection,"
Ella said and sighed.

"Ogre toenails?"
Owen closed his book
and sat up in his bed.
"Oooh! *Now* I want to go!"

The excitement of the
toenails made his nose twitch.
Then twitch again. Then *"AH-CHOO!"*
Fire shot from his nose, and the force
of the sneeze threw him across the room.
He bounced off the wall and tumbled
across the cave.

Owen rubbed his nose with his tail. "Just one question. What's the name of this dragon wizard guy?"

"Dragon Wizard Orlock Morlock. He lives in a cave," Ella said.

"Does the cave have a name?" Owen asked.

"Nope," she said.

"Not possible," Owen replied. "All caves have names, according to the Cave Naming Rules of Sir Stonecastle Rockhound. Like, there's the Cave of Evil Bunny Rabbits, the Cave of Evil Fairies, the Cave of Evil Unicorns. . . ."

"Those creatures don't sound very friendly," Ella said.

"Uh, *yeah*. Why do you think they live in *caves*?" Owen answered.

"Well, this place is just called the, uh, Cave of, uh, Caves," Ella explained. "Because it's a cave full of caves. That aren't evil."

"I don't know." Owen began to have second thoughts. "It sounds kinda iffy. . . ."

"Ogre toenails!" Ella reminded him with a hopeful smile.

Owen got excited again. "What are we waiting for? Let's go!"

The two rushed from their cave, wings flapping.

Ella didn't tell Owen that she made up the name the Cave of Caves. She also didn't tell him the cave was *really* called the Cave of Aaaaah! Doom!

But don't worry. Owen figured that one out soon enough.

② GULPING GRUMPKINS

The trail disappeared into the forest. The dirt path was long gone, covered in weeds. As they walked, the twins heard an animal howl nearby.

"We're lost, aren't we?" Owen asked.

"I did *not* get us lost!" Ella said defensively.

"This is what I get for following you," Owen huffed.

"I'll have you know that I'm using my . . . uh . . . using my cave-finding dragon skills to find the Cave of Caves!" Ella exclaimed.

"Dragons don't have cave-finding skills," Owen said. "You're making that up."

"Quiet please. I will first use my sense of dragon smell to find the trail. . . ."

"We don't have dragon smell," Owen said.

"*Shhh* . . . the cave is this way," she said as she pointed straight ahead.

Thinking quickly, Ella picked up a rock and held it to one ear. "Now I will hold up this rock and listen to what it says. . . ." she said.

"I think that's only for seashells down at Firebreather Beach," Owen said.

"Shhh," she shushed. "It's telling me the way." Ella pointed forward. "There!" she said.

"You expect me to believe that?" Owen asked.

"The rock speaks the truth," Ella said.

Owen reluctantly followed Ella deeper into the forest. They went past the dragonberry bushes, over Unicorn Bridge, and down into the Forest of Shadows, until the trees blocked out the sun.

Owen looked around. "I think your rock got us more lost than you did."

Ella shook the rock. "It must've lost its power in the forest," she said nervously.

"Great. Now we're even more lost," Owen said, "because of a rock."

"*Shhh* . . . I'm thinking," she said.

Instead of being quiet, Owen shouted, "Ella! Look over there!"

Owen took off, wings flapping. "It's a tree sprite! Being lost just got so much better!"

Fluttering between the branches of an old willow tree was something truly rare. It was a tiny rainbow-colored creature flapping its wings as it moved under the leaves.

"Tree sprite? Really?" said Ella. "Looks more like a water sprite to me."

"It wants to play!" Owen said as he chased the sprite.

The sprite peeked out from around a leaf and then zoomed off.

Owen was about to chase it again, but he realized just in time that he was at the edge of a steep hill. "Whoa! That was close," he said as his claws grasped the edge of the hill. He waved good-bye as the sprite flew away.

Ella ran to catch up, but she crashed into Owen. Together, they fell over the edge.

"We're—" said Owen.

BOUNCE!

"Falling—" said Ella.

BOING!

"Down—" said Owen.

BOING!

"The hill!" said Ella.

BOUNCE!

"OOOMPH!" They tumbled to the bottom and landed in a prickle patch filled with vines. On the vines were bright-green melons that looked like big monster heads.

"Grumpkins!" cried Owen.

"Ooh!" Ella said. "I hear they're delicious!"

"I'm not eating anything that looks like it has a face," said Owen, "even if it *is* a fruit."

"Suit yourself." Ella popped a grumpkin into her mouth and spit the seeds onto the ground. "That's so good it makes my scales shiver."

"Umm . . . I wouldn't eat any more of those," Owen said. He pointed to a sign that said: NO EATING! EXCEPT ME EATING YOU!

Ella ignored her brother's warning. She grabbed another plump grumpkin.

Owen snatched it from her. "Not a good idea," he said.

"But a tasty one," she said.

"But the sign!" Owen said nervously.

NO EATING! EXCEPT ME EATING YOU!

"Signs aren't as yummy." Ella swung her tail around like a whip. She poked the pointy end into the grumpkin and pulled it from Owen.

The long vine attached to the grumpkin pulled back tightly. Ella pulled harder. "It's stuck on something," she said.

Owen followed the vine. It wrapped around a tree branch over their heads. At the end of the vine was a large wooden cage. "Uh, Ella, you should really let go. . . ." he said.

NO EATING!
EXCEPT
ME EATING
YOU!

SNAP!

The vine broke in half.

A cage released and dropped over the two dragons.

"Now you've done it!" Owen squealed. "You got us lost, and now we're trapped—trapped like, well, dragons in a cage in the middle of nowhere."

"You wanted adventure and excitement, right?" Ella said. "This is it!"

"I didn't want either of those things!" Owen grabbed the cage and shook it. "I don't suppose you have any dragon sense for cage-breaking?" Owen asked.

The bushes rustled. The sound of two stomping feet came toward them. A large green creature stepped into the clearing. Flies swarmed around his head. His wart-covered legs poked from his purple shorts. When he spoke, a cloud of belly moths shot past his yellow teeth and filled the air.

"Caught two dragons for lunch! That is what I have done," the ogre said.

"You're serving lunch?" Ella asked.

"I don't think we're his guests," Owen said. "I think *we're* his lunch. . . ."

"**B**ut you can't eat us!" Owen cried out.

"Our scales are tough like tree bark," Ella said. "Our stomachs are full of beetle skeletons, and we taste terrible!" Ella turned and licked her brother. "Blegh! See?! He tastes awful!" she said.

"Sorry, I've been sick," Owen said. "My nose is full of dragon boogers and fire."

Ella and Owen sat in their cage on the floor of the ogre's messy hut. The barefoot ogre stomped over to them. "Osgood Ogresteen. That is who I am," he said. "Of the ogres in Ogreville, I am the mean one. Eating dragons, that's what I do."

Owen looked around the hut. There was a huge cooking pot of bubbling brown goo over a fire. Jars of spices hung from hooks on the ceiling. A stack of old bones was piled against the back wall.

Osgood put on a large chef's hat. He tilted it to the right and then to the left. "You are in big trouble for eating my grumpkins is what you is," he said. "Gimme back the grumpkin you did eat, or into my stew pot goes you."

Ella's eyes widened in shock. "I can't replace the grumpkin. I ate it."

"Suit yourself," said Osgood. "Grumpkin stew, dragon stew—no difference is there to my belly."

"My sister is sooooo, so sorry, Mr. Osgood, sir," Owen said. "She won't do it again."

Osgood plopped spices into his bubbling cauldron. "A sniffle of bat curry, claws dried from a newt, three drops of owl's hoot, two rattles of a snake, and a leg of spider. Oh, and let's not forget fiery lava salt and a splash of scarlet red pepper."

PEPPER

Ella perked up at the mention of the pepper. "Pepper? Did you say pepper?"

"Pepper is fav-fav-favorite for me," the ogre said.

Ella smiled. "Wellll, if you're going to make a cauldron of dragon stew, I know a very secret dragon secret that'll make it the best dragon stew in Ogreburg."

"No!" the ogre said. "Ogreville is where Osgood lives."

"Right! And you could be the king of Ogre-wherever with my cooking secret," Ella replied.

"Tell me this secret stew knowledge!" Osgood said.

"Promise to keep it a secret?" Ella asked.

"All secrets are kept secret with me!" Osgood replied.

"Very well," Ella said. "If you want the yum-yum-yummiest dragon stew, the best thing to do is put a little pepper on the dragon before you cook him."

Osgood grabbed a few pinches of pepper and threw them at Ella.

Ella sneezed. "Don't forget the other dragon. Two's better than one."

Owen backed up in the cage. "Oh no. I'm not a fan of pepper. Really."

"But I am so much a fan of making you yummy to my tummy." Osgood threw a big handful of pepper at Owen. It landed right on Owen's nose.

Owen's nose twitched. His nostrils wiggled. His scales shook and rattled. His tail whipped in a circle. "Woo-woo-woo!" he yelled. He tilted his head back and his whole body shook as he sneezed a blaze of dragon fire. *"AH-CHOO!"* Fire shot out of his mouth and scorched the cage.

Osgood stumbled backward. "*Aaaaah! Dragon fire!*" he shouted.

"*AH-CHOO!*" More fire shot out.

"*AH-CHOO!*" Then even more fire!

"Got to get away from the dragon fire!" Osgood screamed as he opened up a wooden trunk and jumped in, slamming the lid closed.

Ella pushed against the door of their cage. It swung wide open. "My plan worked beautifully!" she said.

"That was a plan?" Owen asked.

"Yup. Now just run and don't stop!" Ella ran for the door of the hut, but Owen stayed put and looked around.

"Hang on!" he said. Owen ran to the ogre's spice shelves and grabbed a jar of ogre toenail clippings.

He paused to think for a second, and then he looked down, popped dragon lint from his belly button, and placed it on the shelf where the jar was. "Good trade!" Owen said. "Thanks, Osgood!"

"Thanks to you for not sneezing fire on me again, oh mighty dragon!" Osgood called out from inside the trunk.

"Who knew ogres were so afraid of fire?" Owen yelled to his sister.

"Run!" Ella yelled.

"No way!" Owen replied. "We've got wings! Let's go!"

Ella and Owen flew out of Osgood's hut
as quickly as they could.

"Thank you for eating me not!" was the
last they heard from the ogre.

When they were safely away, Ella smiled. "Say it," Ella said.

"Nope," Owen replied.

"Come on. Say it," Ella said again.

"Nope," said Owen.

"Just once! You know I earned it!" Ella said.

"Okay! Okay! *Fine!* Thanks for saving my scales, Ella," Owen said. "I did *not* want to end up as dragon stew!"

"Don't worry, bro! There's no way I'm letting anything eat you!" Ella replied. "Mom and Dad would ground me for one thousand years if I did."

With Ella leading the way, the two dragons soon arrived at a dark and creepy cave. A chill shot through Owen's wings as they landed at the vine-covered entrance.

"I told you we'd find it!" Ella cheered.

"Who . . . who told you about this place?" Owen asked nervously.

"A tree elf named Branchy McElffenberry," Ella replied.

Owen peered into the cave. "This place is blacker than Mom's toadstool pie. Are you *sure* this is the Cave of Caves?"

"Sure, I'm sure that I'm sure!" Ella said quickly.

"If this *is* the Cave of Caves, then why does the sign say the Cave of Aaaaah! Doom?!" Owen asked, pointing to an old, broken sign that said the CAVE OF AAAAAH! DOOM! in big red letters underneath a screaming skeleton head.

"Because dragon wizards can't spell!" Ella offered. "Let's get flapping, bro!"

"Swear on your horns that you're telling the truth!" Owen said as he glared at Ella with his yellow eyes.

"Okay, so maybe I sort of, just a teeny tiny little bit, kinda, but not much, didn't tell you the *whole* truth about the cave's name," Ella admitted. "But Branchy McElffenberry said this *is* where the Dragon Wizard Orlock Morlock lives!"

"Aw, dragon scales! I almost got turned into stew for *this*?!" Owen huffed. "I'm going home!"

"AH-CHOO!" A fire sneeze shot from Owen's mouth and sent him flying out of control.

PING!

ZING!

ZOOM!

Owen bounced about like a rubber dragon egg until he smacked into the sign that said the CAVE OF AAAAAH! DOOM! The skeleton head fell off above the sign and bonked him on the head.

"On second thought, lead the way," Owen said as he rubbed his aching head. "I've gotta get rid of this cold."

Owen hid behind Ella as the two dragons tiptoed on their pointy claws and carefully crept into the dark cave.

"Hey, why can't wizards ever live in a place called the Cave of Yay! Fun and Happiness?!" Owen whispered.

"Because that's where all the *fairies* live," Ella whispered back. "And fairies don't like wizards because they steal all their magic fairy flour to make Wicked Wizard Waffles."

The siblings stopped in their tracks as they heard a loud *GROWL!*

"Please tell me that was your tummy rumbling," Ella said.

"No, it wasn't me, because my tummy doesn't have *big, scary eyes!*" Owen shouted and pointed to two huge eyes glowing in the darkness.

Their eyes blinked, and then the siblings heard a cave-rumbling *ROAR!*

Ella and Owen were frozen in fear. They heard another *ROAR!* that echoed through the cave. Something big and square swooped down on them from above. It had brown wings; sharp, stabby fangs; red eyes; and smelled like breakfast.

"AAAAAH! It's a giant Wicked Wizard Waffle!" Ella screamed.

"DOOOOOM!" Owen yelled. He paused for a moment and then said proudly, "Hey! Now we know why they call this place the Cave of Aaaaah! Doom!"

Ella and Owen gave each other a quick glance, and then both yelled, "RUN!"

The panicked dragons flapped their wings to escape. Instead of exiting quickly, they bonked into each other and fell to the ground.

"What do Wicked Wizard Waffles hate?!" Ella asked as the monster waffle swooped toward them.

"Very small puppies?!" Owen asked.

"No!"

"Gnomes!" Owen guessed.

"No!"

"Well they *should* hate gnomes. They're annoying!" Owen said.

"They don't hate gnomes!" Ella replied. "They hate music, so start singing!"

"Pixie bells, ogres smell, vampires hate the day! When a dragon flies and blows its fire, the villagers run away!" Ella and Owen sang as loud as they could.

The Wicked Wizard Waffle covered its
buttery ears and flew from the cave to
escape their horrible singing. The siblings
turned and gave each other a high five.

"I've never been so happy that you sing so terribly!" Ella said, relieved.

But Ella and Owen weren't out of trouble yet!

"Don't move!" someone called out from behind them.

Ella and Owen spun around and came face-to-face with a wizard! It had:

CELERY ARMS!

CARROT LEGS!

A BROCCOLI BODY!

A CAULIFLOWER HEAD!

A POINTY HAT!

It wasn't *just* a wizard! It was an . . .

"EVIL VEGETABLE WIZARD!" Owen screamed. *"AAAAAH! DOOOOOM! AGAIN!"*

"Why did you sing to my Wicked Wizard Waffle?!" the evil vegetable wizard yelled. He pointed his asparagus wand at them. "Tell me why you're here, or I'll use my magic to make a really grumpy pancake!"

"I think he's serious!" Ella said.

"Of *course* he's serious!" Owen replied. "He's a vegetable!"

"We don't want any trouble," Ella explained. "We're looking for the Dragon Wizard Orlock Morlock."

"*I* am the wizard Orlock Morlock!" The vegetable wizard waved his wand in the air to look dramatic.

Owen glared at Ella. "I thought Stumpy McElf-face or whatever his name is said Orlock Morlock was a *dragon* wizard?!"

Ella shrugged her shoulders. "That's the last time I trust a tree elf," she said.

The two dragons were in a cage. *Again.*

Orlock pushed the door closed.

SLAM!

"I'm tired of everyone putting us into a cage!" Ella complained.

The vegetable wizard had taken the two dragons to his wizard dungeon deep in the cave. Torches lit the room. Next to Orlock's workbench was a large statue of a winged lion. On top of the statue was a clear crystal ball. Dozens of magic items hung from the walls, which were covered in slimy moss and smelled like an old shoe.

"What're you going to do with us?" Ella asked.

"Turn you into flying monkeys!" Orlock answered as he rubbed his parsley beard.

"That's not a very nice thing to do!" Ella said.

"They don't call us evil wizards because we do *nice* things!" Orlock sneered.

"Can my wings have racing stripes?" Owen asked.

Ella glared at Owen. "You're not helping!"

"What? At least he's not going to turn us into flying bunny rabbits," Owen said.

Orlock perked up. "Great idea! Flying bunnies are even funnier than flying monkeys!"

"I know how you can make sure we have *huge* bunny ears!" Ella said, thinking quickly.

"If it needs magic fairy flour, don't bother. I used all of mine to make that giant waffle you two chased away," Orlock said.

"Nope. All you need to do is pour some pepper on Owen," Ella explained. "It'll make him grow huge bunny ears bigger than a unicorn's horn."

"Nice try! If I dump pepper on him, he'll sneeze fire, I'd bet. Do you think I'm as dumb as an ogre or something?" Orlock raised his asparagus wand to turn them into flying bunnies.

"Wait!" Owen yelled. "Maybe there's something we could trade you so you'll set us free?"

Orlock thought for a moment, the asparagus wand still held over his head. "Well, there *is* one thing I'd be willing to trade."

"Name it!" Owen said.

"Dragon belly button lint for my lint collection!" Orlock said.

Owen smiled a big smile. "I've got plenty right—"

He looked down at his belly button and his smile faded. He had left all his belly button lint with Osgood the ogre. Owen looked to Ella (who washes her belly button every morning) and sighed. "I hope you like being a flying bunny rabbit."

Owen and Ella hugged each other.

Orlock waved his wand and... **POOF!**
The two dragons grew long bunny ears.

"Uh, we're still more dragon than bunny rabbit," Ella said as she wiggled her fuzzy ears.

Orlock waved his asparagus wand again.

POOF!

Now Ella and Owen had fuzzy bunny tails.

"Nope. Still not bunnies," Owen said.

A frustrated Orlock waved his wand again and again and again.

With each wand wave, Orlock turned
Owen and Ella into dragons with bunny
teeth, dragons with cute pink noses, and
dragons with big white bunny feet. But the
one thing Orlock could *not* turn them into
was plain old bunny rabbits with wings.

"Are you *sure* you're an evil wizard?"
Owen asked.

"Yes! But . . . I'm just terrible at casting
spells! All I can do is turn broccoli into
cauliflower!" Orlock threw his wand to the
ground and started to cry.

Ella and Owen couldn't help but feel sorry for him.

"Don't cry, Orlock. It'll just make you soggy," Ella said.

"Maybe there's some way we can help?" Owen said.

Orlock wiped his tears and picked up his floppy asparagus wand. "It'd help if you could turn my asparagus wand into a rhubarb wand. Those are *really* powerful!"

80

"Um, not really sure how we'd do that ..." Ella looked to Owen, who shrugged.

"We'd need ogre toenails to make the magic potion, but the ogre down the trail always tries to make stew out of me when I go to ask for some," Orlock explained.

"*We* have ogre toenails!" Ella flapped her wings in excitement.

"No way!" Owen hugged the ogre toenails against his chest. "I traded my best belly button lint for these!"

"Give him the toenails!" Ella tried to grab the jar away. "If you do, you can have my dessert for a week!"

"Chocolate-covered caterpillars?" Owen asked.

"Yes!" Ella said and tugged the jar.

"Make it three weeks!" Owen said and tugged it back.

"Two weeks!"

"Deal!"

Owen yanked the jar of ogre toenails from Ella and gave it to Orlock.

"Let's make a rhubarb wand!" Owen said.

8

ORLOCK THE NOT-SO-EVIL WIZARD

Orlock proudly waved his new rhubarb wand in the air!

"It worked! It worked! It worked!" Orlock sang and danced. "I turned my asparagus wand into a rhubarb wand!"

"Remember our deal! We gave you the ogre toenails. You have to let us go! And cure me!" Owen said.

"*And* you have to also stop being evil," Ella added.

Orlock stopped dancing. "Can I still be evil on weekends?" he asked hopefully. "Pleeease?"

"Mondays only," Ella said. "Because everybody already hates Mondays."

"And holidays? You can't expect me to *not* be evil on Evil-mas—" Orlock said.

"Great! Evil on Evil-mas," Owen cut in. "Now please cure me before I—*AH-CHOO!*"

Too late!

BING! **BANG!** **BONK!**

Fire shot from Owen's mouth like a rocket ship blasting off. He bounced around the dungeon like a soccer ball being kicked by ten trolls, before rolling to a stop in front of a jar filled with bat wings.

"You kept up your end of the deal, and now it's time for me to do my part." Orlock pointed his rhubarb wand at Owen. "Oh, and if this turns you into a Prickle Pie Toad, I'm sorry. I'm just not very good with spells."

"Wait!" Owen shouted.

But it was too late! Again!

SHOOM!

A magic glimmer shot from Orlock's rhubarb wand and surrounded Owen. Owen closed his eyes tightly. The magic sparkles went away, but he was not a Prickle Pie Toad. He was still plain old Owen.

"Give it a try," Ella said and tickled Owen's nose.

Owen sneezed . . . but no fire came out!

"Hey! The spell worked!" a surprised Orlock said.

Owen gave his sister a look of relief.

Ella smiled and gave her brother a quick high five.

With Owen cured, the two dragons said their good-byes to Orlock the Evil (on Mondays and holidays only) Vegetable Wizard.

But the journey home wasn't as easy as the journey *to* the Cave of Aaaaah! Doom!

"**W**e need to go left here," Owen said when they came to a fork in the path.

"No, we need to go right," Ella countered.

Every time Ella said "go left," Owen thought they should go right. If Owen said "up," then Ella said "down." If Ella said "backward," then Owen said "forward." If Owen said "peanut butter," then Ella said "jelly."

But the bickering got even worse when they spotted a tiny glowing winged girl no bigger than an ogre's toe.

"Look! It's the tree sprite we met earlier!" Owen waved to her. "Hi, there!" he called out.

"No, that's a water sprite for sure!" Ella replied.

"Tree sprite!"

"Water sprite!"

"Let's go ask!" they both said at the same time.

ZOOM!

They flew toward the sprite, who, seeing two dragons flying toward her shouting "tree sprite!" and "water sprite!" became scared and flew away.

The chase was on!

Just as they were about to grab the sprite, the two dragons crashed into each other.

BAM!

They tumbled down a hill through a patch of spider flowers and sticky slug weeds until . . .

SPLASH!

The twins fell into a cold lake of inky
black water.

"This is all your fault!" they both yelled
at each other at the same time.

But then Ella and Owen looked around and realized something that was very not good.

"Do you have any idea where we are?" Owen asked.

"In a lake?" Ella replied.

"In a lake . . . and completely and totally lost!" Owen replied.

"We're not lost!" Ella said. "Home is . . . that way! Or is it that way? Or . . ." Ella spun in circles, looking in every direction. She realized that they were indeed completely and totally lost. "I hate it when you're right. . . ." she said with a sigh.

And Owen was right. They were more lost than a dwarf without a beard. . . .
Uh-oh!

TABLE OF CONTENTS

"**W**e are *not* lost!" Ella said to her twin brother as they swam through the water.

"Right," Owen said. He gave his sister a blank look. "We just fell down a big hill, splashed into this lake, and don't know our way home."

"You say that like it's a bad thing," Ella replied. "Don't worry. My dragon sense will lead the way."

"Dragon sense? Ha!" Owen laughed.

"My dragon sense led us to Osgood the ogre and also the Cave of Aaaaah! Doom! and the Wizard Orlock Morlock, who cured your cold," Ella said proudly. "Just like I promised."

"You say that like it was a good thing!" Owen said. "Your dragon sense also got us into this mess and—whoa!" Owen flipped his tail out of the water. He looked behind himself nervously. "Something swam past me. Something BIG!"

"Don't be sil—*EEEEE!*" Ella screamed. "There *is* something in the water!" She began bobbing up and down.

"Maybe it's a friendly fish," Owen said hopefully. "A big friendly fish that wants to be friends because it's so friendly."

SPLASH! Suddenly, a huge Black Water Slime Eel jumped out from the water behind them. Its mouth snapped open. Giant fangs stuck out like tusks. Its angry scream sounded like an alarm. It was coming right at them.

"FLY AWAY!" Ella and Owen cried out at the same time.

Their dragon wings flapped as fast as wings can flap. They flew above the lake and—**BONK!** Ella and Owen crashed into each other.

SPLASH! They fell back into the water. The slime eel's back fin rose from the water like a sword. Its mouth opened, and it spit out the bones of a smaller fish. Huge fangs sparkled in the sun. Owen and Ella dove out of the way. The eel swam past, missing both of them.

"Grab the fin!" Ella yelled.

"No way!" Owen said. "That's crazy!"

Ella stretched her scaly arm and grabbed the slime eel's tail. "Follow me!"

"I'm too far away!" Owen yelled. "All I can grab is—" Owen grabbed Ella's tail.

The slime eel swam away fast, pulling Ella through the water. Owen hung on tightly.

"Stop tugging on my tail!" Ella yelled back to her brother.

"I'm trying to save you!" Owen shouted.

"That's so nice of you, but this is great! I'm a dragon cowgirl," Ella yelled. *Yippee-ki-yay!*"

Then the slime eel lifted its tail out of the water and snapped it like a whip. Ella and Owen flew off the eel and headed toward the shore.

"*AAAAAH!*" they screamed as they sailed through the air.

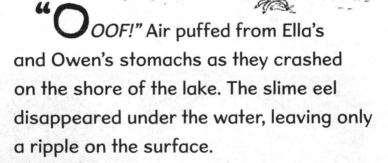

"*OOOF!*" Air puffed from Ella's and Owen's stomachs as they crashed on the shore of the lake. The slime eel disappeared under the water, leaving only a ripple on the surface.

"See? That worked out great!" Ella said.

"Sure, if you like to eat sand," Owen said as he spit out a bunch of sand along with his forked tongue.

Ella shook the sand from between her scales. She pointed to a light in the distance. "Hey, Owen, is that the sprite we were chasing?"

"Do you mean the whole reason why we ended up in the lake in the first place? I don't care. I'm *not* going that way," Owen said. "I'm going the other way."

"Why?" asked Ella.

"Because every time I've chased that sprite, I've gotten lost or fallen down a hill or gotten thrown in a cage or almost gotten eaten! *This* way has to be better!" Owen pointed in the opposite direction of the light. He marched off, snout in the air. "This. Way." Then he tumbled down a hill. *"YAAAAAA!"*

BOUNCE!
"OUCH!"
BOUNCE!
"OOOF!"
BOING!
"OUCH—OOOF!"

Ella leaned over the top of the hill and yelled down, "Owen! How's that other way working out?" She leaned too much, though. Then she tumbled down the hill as well. "YAAAAAA!"

BOUNCE!
"OUCH!"
BOUNCE!
"OOOF!"
BOING!
"OUCH—OOOF!"

She landed on top of Owen. "Thanks for breaking my fall. You're as soft as a bag of weaselbird feathers."

"Sure . . . feathers . . . *OOOF . . .*" Owen coughed, and Ella rolled off of him.

"Any idea where we are?" Ella asked.

"What? You don't know?" Owen replied. "Maybe I have *your* dragon sense. *I* know where we are!"

"How do you know that?" Ella asked

"Because we live over *there*!" Owen pointed toward a nearby path.

Ella saw that Fright Mountain was not that far away. She shrugged, acting as if she knew they were just minutes from their cave. "Race you!" Ella said.

"I'm halfway there already!" Owen flapped his wings and flew over the rocky trail.

Ella caught up quickly and passed her brother, but Owen stretched out his snout as far as it could go.

"Winner!" He skidded to a stop just as the front door to their cave opened up.

"Well, there you are!" their mother, Goldenrod, said.

"Mom! Dad!" Ella said.

"We're home!" Owen added.

"I'm glad to see the fresh air got rid of your cold," their mom said.

"Don't ask how," Owen mumbled. He stared at Ella, who smiled back.

"We're just on our way out," their father, Daryl, said.

"Where are you going?" Ella asked.

"If you're chasing a tree sprite, let me stop you right now. . . ." Owen said, still out of breath.

"Only a fool chases a tree sprite," Daryl said.

"Your father is such a romantic!" Goldenrod explained. "We're going out to scare the people in town."

Ella gave her parents a confused look. "You guys never do that kind of stuff anymore," she said.

A brief look of embarrassment crossed Daryl's face. "We know. It's not the *nicest* thing to do, but we're only looking to slightly scare the villagers," he said. "They *do* live right near Fright Mountain after all. . . ."

Ella and Owen both nodded, knowing how the villagers pretended that dragons didn't live nearby.

"Today is a special day for your mom. I'm taking her out as a special treat," Daryl explained.

"It's my birthday!" Goldenrod proudly said. "Isn't your father the sweetest?"

"Aww, you deserve it, my scaly beauty," Daryl said. He turned to Owen and Ella and whispered into their pointy ears. "You guys *did* remember that it's your mom's birthday, *right*?"

"Of c-c-course!" Ella stammered. "We'd *never* forget such an important day for Mom!"

"You betcha," Owen lied. "Yep. In fact, we got her the best gift ever!"

"Good!" Daryl whispered. "You can give it to her when we get back. She'll be *so* excited!"

"Are you ready, honey?" Goldenrod asked excitedly as she tapped her claws on the ground.

"Yep! Let's go!" said Daryl. "On three. One . . . two . . . *three!*"

Goldenrod and Daryl zoomed into the sky. Ella and Owen waved good-bye as their parents' long scaly tails disappeared into the clouds.

As soon as their parents were out of sight, Ella and Owen turned to each other and gasped. Their eyes went wide. Smoke puffed from their nostrils in a panic. *"I TOTALLY FORGOT TODAY WAS HER BIRTHDAY!"* they said at the same time.

"We've gotta get Mom a birthday gift!" Ella said.

"And fast!" Owen said. "Got any ideas?"

3
OFF TO SEE A WIZARD

"**O**kay—think!" Ella said to Owen as they walked through downtown Dragon Patch.

"I *am* thinking," Owen replied. "But what do you get your mom for her birthday when it's too late and you've forgotten?"

"I don't even have enough Dragon Ore to buy a new claw polisher," Ella said.

"Or a pearl-handled nose brush to clean out the dust from all the fire-breathing I did when I was sick," Owen said.

"Ewww," said Ella. "Let's try not to remember those sneezes, okay?"

Walking through Firebreather Square, they passed Fairy Frieda's Fairyland Diner, the Troll Market, the Minotaur Theatre, and Ye Olde Five Dwarves Repair Shoppe. A singing sword named Steve sang for vegetables, and an angry elf named Butterfingers offered to hit anyone on the head with his bashing mallet in return for a silver coin.

As they passed the Blind Bat's Baking Boutique, the smell of the baker's special claw and tomato cake gave Ella an idea.

"Cake!" Ella said. "We'll bake Mom a special cake! A newt cream cake with frosted toadstools."

"Great idea!" Owen agreed. "But I think a stinky fish cake with extra stinky fish on top and more stinky fish wrapped around the side would be even better."

"Newt cream!" Ella said.

"Stinky fish!" said Owen.

"Newt cream!"

"Stinky fish!"

They stopped arguing and stared at each other. Then both Ella and Owen said the same thing. *"TWO CAKES!"* they yelled.

Owen took off and ran inside Gorgon Goblin's Stinky Fish Emporium, the stinkiest fish shoppe in Dragon Patch (or so the sign claimed).

"Pee-YEW!" Owen said. "This place smells terrible! I love it!"

"Ugh! This place smells like an old dragon's ear wax." Ella sniffed the air again. "Mixed with the underarm hair from a swamp rat."

"Beautiful, isn't it?!" Owen took a deep sniff. "I could smell it all day long!"

"Are ye a'smellin' or a'buyin'?" asked Gorgon Goblin, the orange-and-tan shop-keeper.

Gorgon hopped on top of a large glass display case. Fish of different sizes and colors lined in ice were brought in from the top of Fright Mountain.

"We're buying, Mr. Gorgon Goblin, sir. A stinky fish, please," Owen requested. "Your stinkiest."

Gorgon reached into his display case. "You have chosen well, dragon boy," the fish seller said. He picked up a blue-and-orange grossfish and dropped it into a paper bag. He took a big whiff of the bag before sealing it. "Delicious! I keep several of these in my bathroom."

"That's too much information," Ella said. She turned to Owen. "Can we get my newt now?"

Owen paid for the grossfish with a piece of Dragon Ore. Gorgon licked it to make sure it was real and tossed it in the crate on the floor. "Have fun with the grossfish! They're even stinkier when they're cooked."

"This day just keeps getting better!" Owen said, smiling from ear to ear.

As they left Gorgon Goblin's Stinky Fish Emporium, Ella stopped and turned to her brother. "Umm—you need to walk behind me. Far, far behind me. Because *pee-YEW!*"

Ella waved her hand in front of her face as Owen walked behind her. He ignored his sister and instead tried to get a whiff of the grossfish inside the bag.

BA-BAM! Ella knocked on the door of the Olden Tyme Spells and Curses Depot. The door creaked open, and they stepped inside. A large puff of lime-green smoke filled the space in front of the twins.

"I am the great wizard," the great wizard said as he stepped out of the smoke. He wore a bright blue robe tied around his waist with a piece of rope. A ragged wizard's cap was on his head, covering a mass of gray hair. In his left hand, he held a bent wooden stick with a star tied to one end.

"The great wizard known by the ancient name of . . . Ken," the wizard said.

"Ken?" Ella asked. "Your name is *Ken*?"

"That doesn't sound like much of a wizard's name," Owen said.

"Blame my parents," the crusty old wizard replied.

Owen shook his head. "You need a cool wizardy name that's full of wizardness, like Wizard Zappo Wandacornium."

"And *you* dragony dragons should buy something or get out of my store," Ken snarled. "Before I curse you!"

Ella turned toward Owen and whispered, "More like Wizard Grumpo Grumpacornium."

Wizard Ken raised his magic wand. "Stop that whispering before I—whoa! What is that *horrible* smell? Have dragons never heard of soap and water?"

"It's the stink of my stinky fish," Owen said, holding his bag proudly in front of him.

Three trolls who walked through the door suddenly pinched their noses. "Ugh! This place smells terrible!" one troll said. "Let's go to Wally Wizard's Wizardly Wands and Pancakes!" said another troll as they stomped out of the store.

Ken stared at Ella and Owen. "Those were my best customers!" he said angrily.

"Don't worry. We're your new best customers," Ella said. "We'd like a newt."

"A newt?" Ken repeated. "A NEWT?!" The wizard pulled out his wand. "You stink up my store and send my customers running away for a measly newt?! I should turn *you* into a newt!"

Ken waved his wand in a circle. The star on top was covered in a swirl of magical energy. He swung the wand toward Ella.

"BAM-A-KAZAM!" Ken shouted, and then he whispered, "Oops."

The star on the top of the wand flew off the handle.

Owen ducked. The magical star sailed over his head and hit a cage on a shelf. The cage snapped open. Huge hairy spiders scampered out.

Ken ran across the room, jammed the star back onto his wand, and began casting more spells at Ella and Owen.

ZAP! ZAP! ZAPPITY-ZAP!

Magical bolts shot across the store. Ella and Owen ducked and dodged.

ZAPPITY-ZAP! ZAP!

The sparkly bolts hit cages and crates, busting them open. Eels slithered out. Three-winged bats flew across the store. Glass tanks of rainbow mice broke open. Bowls of ogre nail clippings emptied. Then Ella spotted a newt scurrying across the wooden floor.

She ran quickly to grab the newt, careful to avoid Ken's zapping wand bolts. *"AH-HA!"* Ella yelled. "Got one!" Ella picked up the newt and tossed a piece of Dragon Ore on the counter. "Let's go, Owen! We have cakes to make!"

On the way out, Ella nearly tripped over the stinky fish bag. "Owen! You dropped your grossfish!" She looked around the store. No Owen. She grabbed the bag and ran out.

Outside the store, Ella looked all around and realized Owen was not with her. "Owen!" she yelled.

"I'm right here!" she heard Owen's voice say.

Ella looked in her hand. At the end of her claws was the newt she'd caught.

"It's me—Owen," the newt said. "I got hit by one of Ken's magic bolts. He turned me into a newt! *A newt!*" He sneezed a little newt sneeze. "And I'm allergic to myself!"

"Great," Ella said, "but can I use you in my birthday cake?"

"NO!" Owen the newt replied. Then he ate a bug. "Hmm. Not bad," he said.

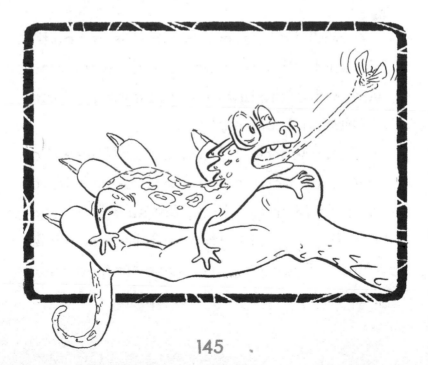

5

TWO NEWTS AREN'T BETTER THAN ONE

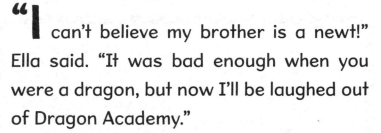

"**I** can't believe my brother is a newt!" Ella said. "It was bad enough when you were a dragon, but now I'll be laughed out of Dragon Academy."

"Don't worry," Owen said. "There's a pixie shop across the street. Pixies have all kinds of magic junk. I'm sure they can help me," he said. They entered the Pixie Wishes Shoppe and were immediately greeted by a green glittery pixie.

146

"Greetings to you!" she said to Ella. "My name is Penelope Pepperpie. You can call me Penelope Pepperpie!" Then Penelope Pepperpie noticed the newt in Ella's paw. "Ah, I see you have brought me a beautiful, beautiful newt! He will make an excellent stew. How much do you want for him?"

"He's not for sale," Ella replied. "I want you to turn him back into my brother."

Penelope Pepperpie took a closer look at Owen and said, "Did you try Ken the wizard? He's very good with newt magic."

Owen's tail curled. "He's the one who turned me into a newt!"

"Can *you* change him back into a dragon?" Ella asked.

"*Oooh!* I love transformation spells! They are, like, *so* much fun to do!" Penelope Pepperpie clapped her little pixie hands.

"So you'll help us?" Ella asked.

"Of course! And it'll only cost ten Dragon Ores!" Penelope Pepperpie said.

"*TEN?!*" Ella gasped. "That's our whole allowance for a month! Isn't there something else we can do?"

"Well . . . I suppose you could do me one little, teeny-tiny, itty-bitty, not-big-at-all favor," Penelope Pepperpie began.

"What kind of little, teeny-tiny, itty-bitty, not-big-at-all favor?" Ella asked.

"Just say yes!" Owen insisted. "My skin is starting to dry out!"

"A delivery," Penelope Pepperpie said.

"Deal!" Owen snapped.

"Great! Please deliver this batch of fresh pixie dust to Wizard Ken." Penelope Pepperpie handed Ella a small sack of pixie dust. Magical sparkles swirled around the top of the sack.

"*WHAT?!*" cried Ella.

149

"You're joking, right?" Owen asked. "Did you not just listen to our story? He turned me into a *newt*! We can't go back there!"

"Well, *I* can't go there," Penelope Pepperpie said. "That grumpy old grump always tries to turn me into a toad, and I *must* make this delivery. Apparently two of his customers caused trouble and now his whole shop is a mess! He needs extra magic to clean it all up."

Owen quickly pictured his life as a newt and then shook the thought out of his head. "We'll do it," Owen said with a sigh.

"Okay, if you say so," Ella said, looking her brother in the eye. She took the bag of pixie dust from Penelope Pepperpie. "We're off to see the wizard," she said.

They walked down to the Olden Tyme Spells and Curses Depot. Owen sat on one of Ella's shoulders as they walked in and she tiptoed across the wooden floor. "So far, so good," she whispered to her tiny brother.

Until the floor creaked.

Then Wizard Ken rushed out from the back room. *"YOU!"* he shouted and waved his wand over his head. "I warned you!" Bolts and zaps shot across the room.

Moments later two newts ran out the front door of the Olden Tyme Spells and Curses Depot. Two newts named Owen and Ella.

"This is all *your* fault!" they shouted at each other.

"I only promised to turn *one* of you back to normal if you made the delivery," Penelope Pepperpie explained. "But now that Ken has turned *both* of you into newts. . . ."

Ella and Owen were back at the pixie's shop. They were still newts, and Penelope Pepperpie was still a pixie. That had nothing to do with Ella and Owen still being newts, but it's always good to know who was still what when a grumpy wizard like Ken was zapping his wand at everyone.

"Then turn Ella back into a dragon," Owen said as he bravely puffed out his little newt chest.

"You're a very kind brother. You deserve a treat." Penelope Pepperpie reached into one of her cabinets and then fed Owen a beetle.

"Nah, I just can't wait to see how much trouble Ella's gonna get in when Mom and Dad find out that I'm a newt!" Owen laughed and gulped down the bug.

"Either we're both dragons or we're both newts, and I don't want to be a newt, so do you know what *that* means?" Ella asked.

"That I get all your bugs?" Owen scampered up the wall and onto the ceiling. "Hey! Being a newt is kinda cool!"

Penelope Pepperpie's wings fluttered like a green butterfly and flicked sparkly green glitter all over the store. "Okay, I'll turn you *both* back if you deliver another package for me." She put a smaller bag of pixie dust on the counter. "Bring this to Wizard Ken. He just ordered more."

"Tails and snails! We are *not* going back there!" Ella said. "Who knows what he'll turn us into this time?!"

"I hope it's *not* something with four heads!" Owen said.

Then . . . *PLOP!*

Ella heard something fall next to her.

In all the excitement, Owen accidentally fell off the ceiling and landed next to his sister. "That was close!" Owen said. "I almost squashed you, Sis!"

"We can't go back to Ken's shop. Is there anything else we can trade you to turn us back into dragons?" Ella asked.

"I'll give you all my ogre toenails," Owen offered.

"Nah," Penelope Pepperpie replied.

"Owen will give you all his dried bat wings," Ella offered.

"Nope," Penelope Pepperpie said.

"I'll give you my collection of fire snails," Owen offered.

"Uh-uh," Penelope Pepperpie replied, turning her head in disgust.

"Owen will give you his collection of lava worms," Ella offered.

"Why do you keep trying to give away my stuff?" Owen asked.

"Because it's not *my* stuff," Ella replied. "Seems like a no-brainer to me."

"Sorry, guys. I don't want any of those things. Pixies like stuff like rainbows and unicorns and rainbows made of unicorns and stinky fish cake and unicorns made of rainbows and—"

"WHAT DID YOU JUST SAY?!"
Owen and Ella both shouted.

"Unicorns made of rainbows?" Penelope Pepperpie asked.

"Before that!" Ella said.

"Stinky fish cake?" Penelope Pepperpie asked.

"Dragon tails! We'll make you a stinky fish cake if you turn us back into dragons!" Ella cheered.

"It's a deal, but only if you make it extra stinky!" Penelope Pepperpie clapped her tiny hands.

"If you wanna make stuff extra stinky, you've come to the right guy!" Owen proudly announced.

Penelope Pepperpie wiggled her ears and tossed a handful of pink glitter at Owen and Ella.

POOF! They were instantly covered in a sparkly cloud, and when the air cleared, Ella and Owen were dragons again!

"I'm so happy that I could hug you!" Ella cheered.

"Ugh! I'd rather be a newt!" Owen blew fire from his mouth to keep all possible hugs far away.

Penelope Pepperpie handed Ella a bag of pixie dust. "Please sprinkle a very, very, very little, teeny-tiny  bit on the top of my stinky fish cake to make it glitter! Because, you know, pixies *love* glitter!"

The two dragons thanked the giggly little pixie and rushed toward home . . . but not before Owen ate one last beetle.

"The taste kinda grows on you," he said. He grabbed the bag with the grossfish inside and followed his sister out the door.

"I've got the slime!" Ella called out.

"I've got the salamander eggs!" Owen called back.

"Here's the worm powder!" Ella added.

"I need more toad warts!" Owen said.

Back at their cave, Ella and Owen rushed to make two stinky fish cakes—one for their mom and one for Penelope Pepperpie.

160

"And last but not least, some grossfish
on top!" Owen said, proud of their work.

Ella whipped out the bag of pixie dust
and sprinkled some onto the second cake.
"There! A very, very, very little, teeny-tiny
bit just like Penelope Pepperpie said."

"Don't we want to make it special for Penelope Pepperpie? She *did* turn us back into dragons," Owen said. He took the bag of pixie dust from his sister and dumped the whole thing onto the cake. "If a very, very, very little, teeny-tiny bit will make the cake glitter, the whole bag should make it light up like fireworks!"

BOOM! The cake exploded and the kitchen turned into a cloud of pixie dust and cake pieces. The explosion had ruined both cakes, and covered Ella and Owen in bits and pieces of cake.

"Nice going, Bro," Ella said. She brushed some cake pieces off her wings. "Got any more bright ideas in that scaly head of yours?"

"Yes," Owen replied, staring at what used to be their cakes. *"RUN!"* he yelled.

A loud roar filled the room!

The huge amount of pixie dust had turned the stinky fish into a giant stinky fish monster . . . and it was hungry! It had blue-and-orange fish scales, two short legs, and a huge mouth, big enough to swallow Ella and Owen in one fishy gulp! Worst of all was its odor! *Pee-yew!* It smelled worse than Owen after a week without a bath!

Ella and Owen flew from their cave as quickly as their little wings could carry them. The stinky fish monster stomped after them, its fishy mouth chomping at their tails.

"That thing's trying to eat us!" Owen shouted.

"It's only fair," Ella said as they flew for their lives. "We were going to eat him first, but I have a plan! We have to get that stinky fish monster to Wizard Ken!"

"Back to the wizard?!" Owen gasped. "You're worse than that pixie Pepperpie Pooppip Pipeapoo—or whatever her name is! That's the kinda plan a bridge troll would make up!"

"*BLAAAAAARG!*"

The stinky fish monster blaaaaaarged and covered Owen in slimy fish monster slobber.

"On second thought, I love your idea!" Owen said, wiping off his wings. "Let's go!"

They flew toward downtown Dragon Patch and . . . watched as the stinky fish monster ran the other way toward the lake.

"It's getting away!" Ella panicked.

"It's not getting away—*we're* getting away!" Owen corrected.

"Quick! Fly after him! He has to chase us!" Ella said.

"What? Did you breathe fire on your little brain or something?" Owen couldn't believe it. "Why would we do that?!"

"Because it's part of the *plan*!" Ella replied.

"Then let's make up a *new* plan where the fish monster that's *trying* to eat us *doesn't* eat us because it disappeared into a lake instead!" Owen shouted.

Ella didn't answer. She was too busy shouting at the stinky fish monster. "Hey, stinky fish monster! Come eat my brother!"

"What? Why me?" Owen complained.

"If you don't want to get eaten, make up your own plan next time," Ella said.

The stinky fish monster stopped. It turned and glared at Owen with its scary yellow eyes.

"Look at m-m-me. So t-t-tasty," Owen stammered and then licked his arm. "Mmm-mmm g-g-good."

The stinky fish monster licked its fat pink lips with a gooey purple tongue and then leaped at Owen.

"AAAAAAAH!" Owen screamed and flew away with Ella.

The stinky fish monster roared and chased them down the path toward Wizard Ken's shop.

THREE CHEERS FOR WIZARD GRUMPO GRUMPACORNIUM

GLARG! BLARG! PLARG!

The stinky fish monster glarged, blarged, and plarged as it stomped through the narrow streets of downtown Dragon Patch, trying to catch its dinner, which just happened to be named Owen and Ella.

"You got yourself a mighty stinky pet!" a fairy named Dewdrop said to Ella and Owen.

"It's not our pet!" Ella blurted out as they flew past.

The stinky fish monster roared at Dewdrop. She quickly flew into Ye Olde Five Dwarves Repair Shoppe and hid in a dwarf's beard.

The creatures of downtown Dragon Patch screamed and raced to safety. Trolls hid under bridges, witches flew away on brooms, and elves climbed trees to escape.

"Sorry, folks! Show's over!" Steve the singing sword yelped and hopped away on his hilt the moment he saw the stinky fish monster.

"Where is this monster?! I'll bash him back to Stinky Swamp!" Butterfingers the angry elf shouted and waved his bashing mallet over his head.

GULP! The stinky fish monster swallowed Butterfingers's bashing mallet in one gulp. He would've swallowed Butterfingers in one gulp as well if the elf hadn't run away screaming.

"Hey! Over here!" Ella yelled to the stinky fish monster so he'd chase them again.

The stinky fish monster jumped at them and grabbed Ella's tail in its mouth.

"*OOOOOOO-WEEEEEEN!*" she yelled.

"Is this part of your plan, too?" Owen gasped as he struggled to pull her free.

"*PULL!*" Ella shouted.

Owen pulled with all his dragon might. Ella's tail popped free of the stinky fish monster's mouth, and the two tumbled to a stop outside Ken's Olden Tyme Spells and Curses Depot.

"Perfect! We're here!" Ella said.

"Ugh! What's that smell?" Ken stormed from his shop. "You two again?" he shouted the moment he saw Owen and Ella in a heap on the ground. "This time I'm gonna turn you two pests into Pink-Bottomed Burping Bugs!"

"I bet you're not a good enough wizard to turn us into a glittery stinking fish cake!" Ella said.

A furious Ken whipped out his wand. "I could do that with my eyes closed!"

The stinky fish monster, which was right next to Owen, opened its huge mouth to swallow the dragons.

"Less talking, more wand zapping!" Owen yelped.

ZAP! A bolt of magic shot from Ken's wand. Ella flapped her wings and barely avoided the blast.

BLAMMO! It was a direct hit to the stinky fish monster. It went from being a horrible creature trying to eat Ella and Owen to a delicious glittery dessert, but it was still stinky.

"You won't dodge me this time!" Ken aimed his wand at Ella and Owen.

There was no escape, so the two dragons did what any brother and sister would do before a grumpy wizard turned them into a glittery stinking fish cake. They pointed a finger at each other and shouted . . .

"IT'S ALL HER FAULT!"
"IT'S ALL HIS FAULT!"

Then, just as it looked like Ella and Owen might be turned into stinky desserts themselves, the downtown Dragon Patch townsfolk rushed over and lifted Ken into the air.

"You saved the town!" a dwarf with a red beard down to his feet yelled to Ken.

"Three cheers for Wizard Zappo Wandacornium!" Owen cried out.

"My name is Ken!" Ken shouted, but no one cared.

"Wizard Zappo Wandacornium! Wizard Zappo Wandacornium! Wizard Zappo Wandacornium!" the crowd cheered.

"Stop calling me that! My name is *KEN*!" Ken protested.

"Let's hear it for Wizard Grumpo Grumpacornium!" Ella yelled.

"Hooray for Wizard Grumpo Grumpacornium!" ogres, elves, gnomes, fairies, and trolls cheered as they carried Ken down the street. "Wizard Grumpo Grumpacornium! Wizard Grumpo Grumpacornium! Wizard Grumpo Grumpacornium!"

Ella grabbed the cake. "Come on! Mom and Dad will be home any minute!"

"Oh! Is that my stinky fish cake? I love it!" Penelope Pepperpie squealed as she fluttered over.

"But we need it for—" Owen started to say.

"Love it! Love it! Love it!" Penelope Pepperpie continued.

"We have to give it to—" Ella said.

"It's perfect with a capital *Pixie*! Thanks for making it for me. Our deal is done!" Penelope Pepperpie grabbed the cake from Ella, and she disappeared in a cloud of purple pixie dust.

"Aw, dragon scales!" Ella growled. "She took our only cake! We needed it to give to Mom!"

"I know! And she didn't even ask me if I wanted a slice!" Owen grumbled.

t5 **E**lla and Owen flew back to their cave as fast as they could. They wiped down the kitchen so there were no signs of exploded cake. When the last spot was cleaned, Ella turned to her brother with wide eyes. "We've got no cake for Mom and no time to get anything!" she said. She looked around nervously, searching for *something* to give their mom.

"We don't need a cake. I've got a backup plan!" Owen whipped out his backup plan and proudly showed it to Ella. "Go ahead," he said. "You can thank me now."

"You're kidding, right? That's just a pinecone with mustard on top," Ella said, squinting at the object in Owen's hand.

"Don't knock it until you try it!" Owen took a bite and then spit it out. "*Blech!* Okay, knock it all you want. That thing tastes *terrible!*"

"It's been *so* long since we scared villagers like that. . . ." someone said just outside their cave.

"MOM!" Ella and Owen shouted.

"Yeah . . . good times," they heard someone else say.

"DAD!" Ella and Owen shouted. Again.

"Hey, kids! How's it flapping?" their dad asked as he flew into the cave with their mom. "Is there anything you want to say to your mom?"

"There sure is!" Ella said and whipped out Owen's pinecone with mustard—with a bite taken out of it. "Happy birthday, Mom! We love you! Gotta go!"

"Is that a pinecone with mustard on top?" their mom asked.

"Don't knock it until you try it." Ella chuckled.

"Very funny, kids," their dad said.

Ella and Owen looked at each other guiltily. Ella felt terrible. Owen felt miserable. They *wanted* to give their mom a present on her special day.

"We went to get a present in downtown Dragon Patch, but Wizard Zappo Wandacornium didn't like my stinky fish, so he turned me into a newt!" Owen started babbling.

"And Penelope Pepperpie wouldn't turn him back unless we made a delivery to Grumpo Grumpacornium, but he turned me into a newt, too!" Ella rambled.

"And Pickadoo Porcupine wanted us to make a second delivery, but we traded a stinky cake that we didn't have to Penelope, but I poured too much pixie dust!" Owen was babbling even faster.

"And the fish tried to eat us because we wanted to eat him. Then Grumpo Grumpacornium zapped him, and then Peter Piper Picked a Peck of Pickled Peppers took the cake. Then Owen made a pinecone with mustard!" Ella rambled even faster than her brother.

"Did you get *any* of that?" their dad whispered to their mom.

"Of course," their mom began. "Cranky old Wizard Ken turned them into newts. Penelope Pepperpie the pixie offered to turn them back in exchange for a stinky fish cake, but Owen used too much pixie dust—you know how much pixies *love* glitter—and the fish turned into a monster and tried to eat them. Then Ella came up with a plan—very clever, dear—to lead the monster to Dragon Patch where they tricked Ken into turning it into a stinky fish cake. Unfortunately, Penelope Pepperpie thought it was a cake for her and took it. So Owen made a pinecone covered in mustard—I love your creativity, honey—to give to me instead."

Their dad stared at their mom in shock.

"What?" their mom asked. "It's a mother's *job* to know what her kids are talking about."

"We're sorry we messed up your birthday, Mom." Ella sighed.

"Messed it up? You got me the best present ever!" their mom said.

"See! I told you she'd like the pinecone!"
Owen said to Ella.

"No, I mean annoying that cranky, old
Wizard Ken!" Their mom laughed. "He's
always so rude to me! I've wanted to singe
that wrinkled old grouch's beard whiskers
for years! But your father won't let me."

"The last thing we need is everyone showing up at our cave with torches and pitchforks, dear," their dad began. "Although . . . your mom's right. Ruffling that nincompoop's pointy hat *is* a pretty good gift. But I'd rather have a stinky fish cake."

"We're on it, Dad! We know a great recipe—sort of—and can make you one!" Ella said.

"No way. I've had enough of downtown Dragon Patch for today—and the rest of my life." Owen snorted. "I've got a stack of books just begging me to read them!"

"We don't need to *buy* a stinky fish in downtown Dragon Patch," Ella explained. "We can go to Terror Swamp and catch one!"

"T-t-terror Swamp?!" Owen stammered. "Who names these places?"

"Maybe Ken's parents," Ella replied. "They're not very good with names, after all. Come on, Bro!"

Ella grabbed a fishing pole and flew from the cave.

"Good-bye, books. I promise to come back and read you . . . as long as nothing in Terror Swamp eats me first." Owen sighed and reluctantly followed his sister.

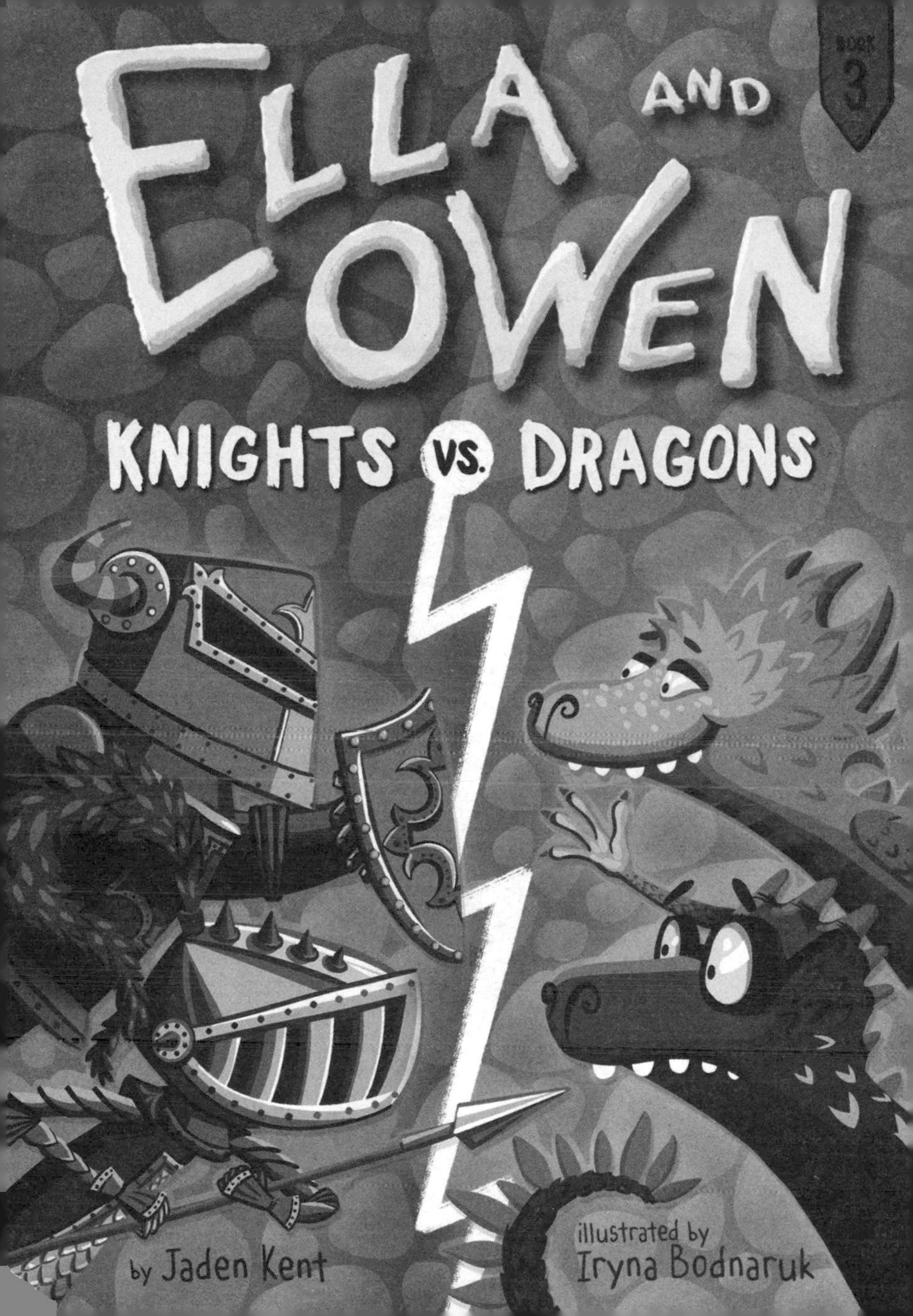
ELLA AND OWEN
BOOK 3
KNIGHTS VS. DRAGONS
by Jaden Kent
illustrated by Iryna Bodnaruk

TABLE OF CONTENTS

"If something in Terror Swamp tries to eat me, I'm totally blaming you," Owen said.

"Me?" his twin sister Ella replied.

"Yes, you!! Going to Terror Swamp was your idea, not mine."

"We can't disappoint Dad," Ella said. "He's expecting a stinky fish, and we're going to catch it for him." The fishing pole over her shoulder swung back and forth as her feet trampled through the forest.

The two dragons had left their home in Dragon Patch that morning with a promise to catch a stinky fish for their father. Unfortunately, as all dragons know, the best stinky fish swim in the muddy waters of Terror Swamp.

"Are you sure this is the way to our doom, I mean, Terror Swamp?" Owen asked.

"It's a shortcut I've heard of," Ella said. "This path through the forest takes us to the other side of Fright Mountain."

"What?! You mean the *wrong* side of Fright Mountain! W-where the k-knights live?!" Owen fearfully exclaimed.

"I've read the books and the scrolls about those knights in that castle, and I've listened to the awful stories from Uncle Scales and Great-Great-Grandmother Clawfoot. Knights hate dragons as much as trolls hate baths." Owen's wings nervously fluttered.

"Don't you wanna see a real castle and a live knight?!" Ella asked.

"Why would I want to meet *anything* that wants to turn my beautiful scaly skin into a pair of dragon boots?!" Owen asked. "I don't want to be boots or shoes or sandals or—"

"Would it be better if they wanted to turn you into a hat?" Ella joked.

"There is *nothing* you can say to change my mind!" Owen huffed. "There's no way I'm going to that castle with you! No way!"

209

"Well, then I guess you'll just have to go back home by yourself," Ella said. "Back through the Fear Forest . . . the Field of Dread . . . and the Sands of Suffering . . . but you know best." Her wings fluttered. "Ta-ta, little brother." She flew off and headed toward the castle. Owen looked around, filled with fear.

"Okay, there's no way you're going to that castle *without* me!" Owen's wings fluttered faster and he took off after his sister.

The two dragons flew through the sky and into the clouds. In just a few minutes, the clouds disappeared, and before Ella and Owen was the castle of the knights who hate dragons.

The castle was made of stone blocks, with a high tower at each corner and a large wooden door.

Across the door was a big banner.

The two dragons landed behind a thick row of bushes near the castle. Owen pushed the branches apart and peeked out.

"Look at all the people in the village," Ella said. "They're singing. It's some kind of festival."

"Check out the banner over the castle door." Owen pointed. "This is our kind of party!"

The banner had only two handwritten words splattered on it: DRAGON DAY.

"I told you the knights weren't so bad," Ella said. "They celebrate dragons."

"Uh, Ella, what's that ugly thing under the banner?" Owen said.

There was a large bag of straw hanging from a rope. Four wooden sticks stuck out from the bag that looked a little like arms and legs. A pumpkin was tied to one end of the bag. Two eyes and a jagged mouth had been carved into it.

"I think that's supposed to be a dragon," Ella replied.

Four knights gathered around the "dragon." Villagers happily danced and stuffed themselves with meat and cheese and bread. An old bard with a long gray beard sat with his mandolin, but didn't play it. "Happy Dragon Day!" the crowd roared. "Happy Dragon Day!"

Owen smiled. "Maybe these humans aren't so bad after all if they have a *holiday* named after dragons!"

"Smash the dragon!" one of the knights shouted.

The villagers stopped dancing. They picked up tomatoes and apples from the festival tables and threw them at the bag of straw. The bard even used his mandolin to bash the fake dragon a few times.

"Happy Dragon Day," he sang.

"Wow," Ella said as they watched from their hiding place. "Worst holiday ever."

2
THE STINKIEST DESSERT OF ALL

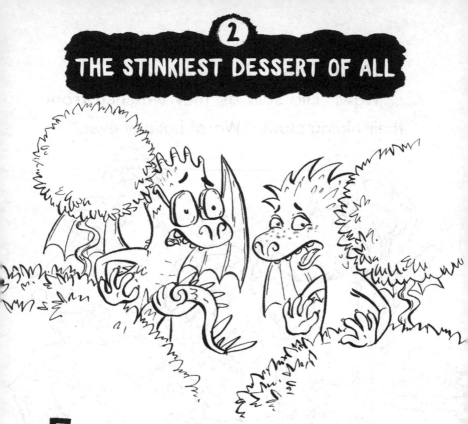

Ella and Owen backed away from the bushes, making sure not to step on a dry twig, rustle any noisy leaves, or trip over their own claws.

"We have to get out of here now," Ella whispered.

But Owen had stopped moving. He was sniff-sniff-sniffing the air.

Owen pointed toward the village feast. Leftovers were stacked on a table.

"Ella! Do you see what I see?!" Owen gasped. "A stinky fish strudel is on that table! It's the best dessert . . . ever!"

Ella shook her head. "I thought you said stinky fish *cake* is the best dessert ever."

"Pffft." Owen rolled his eyes. "Spoken like a dragon who's never had stinky fish strudel. I have a new plan that doesn't involve Terror Swamp." Owen pointed to the fish strudel on the table. "We can just get Dad that stinky fish strudel instead. We'll be heroes and nothing will eat me."

"I think your dragon brain has shriveled!" Ella replied. "That's a terrible idea."

"I know!" Owen said. "In fact, it's such a terrible idea, I'm surprised *you* didn't think it up!"

"Fine," Ella replied. "How do you plan to get your claws into that stinky fish strudel?"

"Easy," Owen said. "By using stealth-dragon tiptoe skills."

"We don't have stealth-dragon tiptoe skills," Ella pointed out.

"I do," Owen said. "I learned them from a book, *101 Ways to Be a Stealth Dragon*. Come on."

Owen tiptoed out of the bushes. He avoided stepping on a dry stick. He did not trip over a small rock. He dodged any prickly sticker cacti.

Ella followed close behind him.

Owen grabbed the stinky fish strudel with his claws, but just as he was about to leave, Ella tapped him on the shoulder.

"Trouble!" she whispered urgently.

The four dragon-smashing knights stomped toward the table.

"HIDE!" Ella and Owen whispered, looking at each other.

The twins scampered under the table. The long tablecloth hid them from the knights.

Owen listened as the knights ate the stinky fish strudel. He wanted to eat it and he wanted to eat it now!

"Can you smell it? It's—it's beautifully stinky!" Owen said. "So stinky beautiful. Stinky. Stinky . . . must have stinky fish strudel!" Owen's eyes were wide with hunger. But the knights were still eating! But the strudel! Could he grab it from the table without getting caught?

One of Owen's shaky hands crawled out from under the table. His claws slid over the table and grabbed a chunk of the stinky fish strudel.

"Yuck! What's with you and food that smells like moldy ogre socks?" Ella asked.

"All the best food smells like moldy ogre socks!" Owen replied. He held the fish strudel up to his open mouth.

Owen gobbled down the stinky fish in one bite and smiled happily.

Then Owen hiccuped.

Then he **BURPED** loud enough to rattle the table.

Ella slapped a hand over Owen's snout. "SHHHHH!" she whispered.

The four knights lifted the tablecloth and stared at the two dragons under their table.

"Behold!" said the first knight. "What's this under our table?"

"Uh . . . Happy Dragon Day?" Ella cracked a weak smile.

"**R**UN AWAY!" Owen shouted.

The table flipped over as Ella and Owen jumped out from underneath it. Food flew into the air. Cups spilled. Plates rattled. The knights jumped back, startled. Ella and Owen ran as fast as their clawed feet could carry them.

Ella huffed and puffed. "You know, we could *fly* away!"

"I-I can't!" Owen replied. "My wings are too scared to flutter!!"

The four knights took off after the dragons. "Get those things!" one shouted.

"Don't let 'em get away!" yelled another.

"Through here," Owen said, pointing at a pair of closed wooden doors of the castle. He crashed into them and bounced off. He tumbled to the ground and stopped in front of Ella.

"Castle doors are pretty strong," Ella said. She pulled the doors open. "And these are pull, not push."

Ella and Owen ran inside the castle. Owen shut the doors behind them.

CRASH! BANG! CLATTER-BA-BOOM!

The knights crashed into the closed doors from outside.

"Curse those running-away-from-us things!" said one knight.

"They have door magic!" said another.

Inside the castle, Ella and Owen scrambled across the courtyard. They ran passed a court jester who shook his rattle at them.

"Riddle me this: Why did the knight cross the road?" the jester asked.

"To get to the other side," Owen said as he and Ella rushed past him.

"To get to the—hey, how did you know that?" the jester exclaimed.

Ella and Owen ran into the nearest castle tower and up the stairs. "Castle towers always have places to hide," Owen said. "At least they do in books."

KLANG! KLANG! KLANG-KLANG!

The footsteps of the knights *KLANG*ed on the stairs.

"They're coming!" Ella said. "Quick—in here!" She opened a door in the tower hallway and ran inside. Owen followed and closed the door behind them.

"Wow." Ella glanced around the room. "Owen, look where we are."

He turned and saw a room filled with swords, axes, spears, mallets, maces, poking sticks, lances, and a number of other pointy weapons that sent a chill up Owen's scales.

"Look over there!" Ella pointed to a row of knights' shiny armor. There were helmets, chest plates, and metal pieces for arms and legs.

"You're thinking of a really bad idea, aren't you?" Owen asked, even though he already knew the answer.

"A *great* idea, you mean," Ella said, smiling.

"Whatever it is, I'm against it," Owen replied.

"We can disguise ourselves as knights and sneak out of here!" Ella said.

"That idea's worse than my idea to get the stinky fish strudel, and *that* was the worst idea I ever had!" Owen said. He burped again. "Even if it was yummy!"

"These are perfect disguises. They'll never know it's us," Ella said.

"Never know?!" Owen cried out. "We're *dragons*! We have *tails*! And do you know what knights hate the most?! Tails! Because they're connected to dragons!"

"Do you have a better idea?" Ella asked.

"We could . . . or we could . . . but . . . then this could . . . or . . . ?"

"Any ideas at all, Owen," Ella said. She handed Owen a shiny metal helmet. "I dub thee Sir Worry-a-Lot."

"Ha-ha," Owen replied. He tried to squeeze his head into the helmet, but it was too small. He pulled and tugged and yanked until it POPPED into place. His snout stuck out from the visor.

Ella took a deep breath and wiggled into a piece of armor that wrapped around her body.

In just a few minutes, they were wearing full suits of armor and looked like large dragons stuffed into small cans.

"You're nuts!" Owen said as they looked at themselves in a mirror.

"Not 'nuts,' *knights*!" Ella said. "We're knights now!"

"You're nuts if you think the knights are nuts enough to think we're knights and not nuts!" Owen said.

"What?" Ella asked.

"I don't know. I didn't really understand it either," Owen confessed. "But you're *still* nuts and we're *not* knights!"

"Now here's the plan," Ella explained. "I'll open the door and we'll just walk out of the castle like we own the place and head to Terror Swamp. No one will know it's us."

Ella gently pushed opened the door. The four knights were standing in the hallway, looking right at them.

"What've we got here?" one of the knights asked.

"**W**hat are you doing in the armory?" said one of the knights.

"He is, I mean we is, I mean we are," Owen stammered.

Ella interrupted. "Hello, friends. This is the brave-knight-who-is-not-a-dragon, Sir Bonehead!"

"And this is Sir Stinky Feet!" Owen said and pointed to Ella. "We're from Not-Dragon-Land."

"It's, uh, very nice to, uh, meet humans like us who are not dragons!" Ella said. "We're just, uh, visiting your castle like knights-who-are-not-really-dragons do."

The four knights glared at Ella and Owen for a moment. Owen's dragon fangs began to chatter. Ella held her fire breath.

"I am Sir Dragon Crusher!" the first knight finally said.

"I am Sir Dragon Stomper!" the second knight proclaimed.

"I am Sir Dragon Thumper!" the third knight revealed.

"Let me guess," Ella said while pointing to the fourth knight, "you're Sir Dragon Masher-Basher-Crasher?"

"Uh, no. My name's Barry," the fourth knight replied. "Welcome to Camelnot!"

"Camel*not*?" Owen asked.

"Yeah! Originally, we were called Camel*lot*, but all the tourists were getting angry because there are no camels here," Dragon Crusher explained.

"So we changed the name to Nocamelot, but no one liked that. So then we tried Camelnotalot, and then Camel-less, Camelnada, Camelnone, Camelzero, No-camels-here-a-lot, Betty, Camelpalooza, and CamelCamel. And in the end, everyone voted for Camelnot."

"Well, that sure explains everything," Owen said.

"You'll love it here in Camelnot!" Dragon Crusher exclaimed. "We have all kinds of great festivals!"

"Like the Summer Festival of Brotherly Love," Dragon Stomper began. "Everyone in the castle gets together and bashes the straw out of a fake dragon!"

"And then there's the Spring Festival of Friendship," Dragon Thumper added. "People come to our castle from villages all across the land and we all smash the straw out of a fake dragon together!"

"But the *best* festival of all is the Winter Festival of Hugs and Kindness," Barry said.

"Ooooh! You're right! That *is* the best one!" Dragon Thumper agreed.

"Because you smack all the straw out of a fake dragon?" Ella asked.

"Don't be silly!" Barry said. "We all share in a great feast and show our kindness and love toward *all* creatures."

"That does sound kinda nice," Owen said.

"And *then* we smack all the straw out of a fake dragon!" Dragon Crusher said.

"Why do you hate dragons so much?"
Ella asked.

"I don't know," Dragon Crusher said with
a shrug. "Maybe because they're all made
of straw?" he added.

"And if we ever, ever see a real dragon,
we'll prove it's made of straw and hate it
even more," Dragon Thumper said.

"We hate whatever they're made of!" Dragon Stomper said.

"I hate dragons because my dad hated dragons," Barry explained. "And my dad's dad hated dragons, and *his* dad hated dragons, and then his dad hated kittens, but *his* dad hated dragons, and . . ."

"And his dad hated dragons. We get it," Ella said with a sigh.

"Actually, his mom hated dragons, but *her* dad hated dragons," Barry said. "Oh, and kittens, too."

"If none of you have ever even met a dragon, why do *you* hate them?" Owen asked.

"Because they're made of straw!" Dragon Crusher replied. "So, duh."

"No one told me there was going to be a test," Dragon Thumper whined.

POP!   POP-POP!

"What was that?" Ella whispered to her brother.

"Don't look now," Owen whispered back, "but your tail is about to pop out of your armor."

"Uh-oh," she exclaimed.

"Thanks, guys! It's been swell, but we gotta fly—I mean run!" Owen said in a panic. He grabbed Ella and pulled her toward the castle gates. "See you later, Dragon Crusher and Dragon Stomper and Dragon Thumper and Dragon Cupid and Dragon Donner and Dragon Blitzen!"

"Where ya going?" Dragon Thumper called out. "We were all gonna go see if there were any princesses locked up in towers by a mean witch and need saving!"

"Uh, we're going to Dragon Patch!" Owen said without thinking.

"Ooooh! We'll come along and help you knock the straw outta them dragons!" Dragon Stomper yelled with a cheer. "That's a lot more fun than saving princesses!"

An annoyed Ella shouted, "Dragons *aren't* made of straw!"

"Pffft. Then what *are* they made out of? *Dragon*?" Barry chuckled.

Before Ella and Owen could make their escape, their knights' armor sprung off their bodies.

Snouts!

Wings!

Tails!

Claws!

Without any armor to hide their bodies, their true selves were revealed.

"Kittens!" Dragon Stomper shouted.

"Those aren't kittens! Those're, uh, um, uh . . ." Dragon Thumper scratched his head.

"Not kittens?" Ella asked.

"That's it! Not kittens! They must be DRAGONS!" Dragon Thumper shouted.

"RUN!" Owen shouted as he and Ella flew from the castle.

"CHASE!" Barry shouted and led the charge.

"We can't lead them back to Dragon Patch!" Owen said as the two dragons flew for their lives. "That'd be a worse idea than disguising ourselves as knights!"

"We need to lose them! What's the one thing knights hate more than anything?" Ella asked.

"Days!" Owen replied. "Get it? 'Cause they're *knights*?" Owen explained.

"Are your scales too scaly?!" Ella asked. "We're being chased by four knights with very long and very pointy swords and you're telling dumb jokes?!"

"Funny jokes!" Owen said.

"Dumb jokes!"

"Funny jokes!"

"DUMB JOKES!" Ella shouted.

The two dragons flapped their wings as quickly as they could, but they couldn't lose the four knights pursuing them on the ground below.

"I know! Let's fly into Terror Swamp!" Ella said.

"That idea is even worse than my last joke!" Owen said.

"It's a *great* idea! Even those knights aren't dumb enough to follow us into Terror Swamp!" Ella happily exclaimed.

"Those sure are some dumb knights," Ella sighed and let out a puff of smoke as the knights followed them into Terror Swamp.

"Aw, dragon scales! What do we do now?" Owen asked.

Ella and Owen landed and were hiding behind a huge pile of moss that began to move.

"Uh, Ella? Why is our hiding place moving?" Owen asked.

"ROAR!" The moss-pile-that-was-not-a-moss-pile howled. Slimy moss arms covered in swamp beetles reached for Ella.

"It's a Beetle-Covered Bog *Moss*-ter!"
Owen shouted.

The green Beetle-Covered Bog Moss-ter
was covered in smelly moss and towered
above Ella and Owen. It looked like a giant
pile of cooked spinach with legs, arms,
and a huge mouth!

"GWAAAAAAAR!" the Beetle-Covered Bog Moss-ter roared as it chased Ella and Owen.

"There they are!" Dragon Crusher shouted the moment he spotted Ella and Owen.

"Dragon tails! Now we've gotta lose a Beetle-Covered Bog Moss-ter *and* four goofball knights!" Owen complained as they fled deeper into Terror Swamp.

"I've got an idea! Follow me!" Ella flew toward a distant light that was barely visible through the swamp vines and trees.

As they flew closer to the light, they realized it was a camp. A *troll* camp to be exact.

"I don't care if those trolls live in the most awesome tent in the world, we are *not* sneaking closer to get a better look," a worried Owen whispered.

"You don't need to tell me twice," Ella said with a gulp.

The two trolls in the camp were big. And ugly. And smelly. And very ugly. And hairy. And very, very ugly. And loud. And very, very, *very* ugly.

A banner that said HAPPY KNIGHTS DAY hung over the campsite. The trolls propped up a scarecrow dressed as a knight and cheered, "Hooray for Knights Day!"

"I'm really starting to think that we live in a very weird place," Owen said. "But what's the plan?"

As if to answer Owen, the Beetle-Covered Bog Moss-ter saw the trolls and fearfully ran in the opposite direction, leaving the dragons alone.

"See! *Everyone's* afraid of trolls!" Ella said.

"Including me!" Owen gulped.

"Now we just need the trolls to scare away those knights," Ella added. "Where are they, anyhow?"

Suddenly, the knights pounced on Ella and Owen, capturing them in a net.

"We got you kittens!" Dragon Thumper said with a chuckle.

"Dragons!" Barry corrected.

"Shhhh!" Dragon Stomper pointed to the HAPPY KNIGHTS DAY banner.

"Knights Day?" Barry read. "What's that?"

"Oh, just a little troll holiday." Ella pointed to the trolls, who kicked around the fake knight as if it were a soccer ball.

"Wow," Dragon Crusher said. "Worst holiday ever."

7
MERRILY WE TROLL ALONG

The sight of the trolls filled the four knights with dread.

"I bet those trolls would never be brave enough to do that to a *real* knight," Ella said, hoping to trick the knights into leaving her and Owen alone so they could escape.

"I know if *I* was a knight, I'd show those ol' trolls they couldn't mess with me," Owen said, with a sly wink to Ella.

The four knights looked at the huge trolls, who were at least twice their height.

"They sure are *big*. . . ." Barry said.

"And ugly . . ." Dragon Crusher said.

"If they're made of straw, we can crush them," Dragon Thumper quietly said in a timid voice. "You go first, Barry."

"I'm *always* going first! You go first, Dragon Crusher!" Barry said.

"I went first last time!" Dragon Crusher protested. "It's Dragon Stomper's turn!"

As the knights bickered about whose turn it was to go first because none of them were brave enough, Ella realized that the trolls had heard them and were coming this way.

"I think this would be a good time to hide!" she whispered to Owen.

The two dragons wriggled free from the net and hid behind a tree.

The four knights stopped bickering when a shadow fell over them. They looked up to see the big, smelly, and very ugly trolls looking down at them.

"What kind of kittens is you?" one troll asked.

"W-w-we're n-not k-kittens. . . ." Barry stammered. "W-w-we're k-k-k-k-k-knights."

"Them is the *worst* kinda kittens!" the second troll yelled with a huff.

"Mommy," Dragon Stomper squeaked.

The trolls snatched up the knights like little dolls and carried them back to their camp.

"Tails and snails! Now we can *finally* go home!" Owen started to fly toward Dragon Patch, but he was the only one in the air. "You know, we can't go home unless we actually *go home*," he said to Ella.

Ella didn't say a word. She just started to collect moss to make a disguise.

Owen slumped back to the ground. "Let me guess. You want us to save the knights from the trolls?"

"Yep," Ella said. "It's part of the Dragon Code."

"We don't have a Dragon Code," Owen replied.

"Well, we should have one," Ella explained. "And rescuing knights is a good way to start."

"Oh, fine!" Owen said, grabbing a handful of moss.

"**Y**ou did it, sis," Owen said as they flew toward the troll camp. "You actually came up with a plan a bazillion times worse than your last one."

Using the moss they had collected around Terror Swamp, the two dragons were disguised as troll fairies.

"We'll just tell the trolls that we're troll fairies and we're here to give them a wish," Ella explained. "And by the time the trolls figure out that we're not, we'll be long gone with the knights."

Ella fluttered into the troll camp. A frightened Owen followed, covering his eyes with his claws.

The four knights were tied to a tree next to the trolls, who were making a huge cauldron of lasagna.

"Oh, helllllllooooooo!" Ella chimed as she glided past one of the trolls. "My name is Sparkly Sparkle Glitter Pop! I'm a troll fairy and I've come to grant you a wish!"

"Me think us should eat it, Dumberdoor," one troll said the moment he saw Ella.

"Me think us should toss it into lasagna and *then* eat it, Dumbdalf," Dumberdoor answered with a grunt.

"B-but I'm a troll fairy! If you eat me, I can't grant you a wish!" Ella cried with a gulp.

"I, uh, thought troll fairies be smelly and ugly?" Dumbdalf asked.

"Have you met my brother, Smelly McUgly the troll fairy?" Ella nudged Owen forward.

"H-hi. I-I-I'm Smelly McUgly the t-t-troll fairy," a frightened Owen stammered.

"Wow, that one ugly and smelly troll fairy," Dumberdoor said in agreement.

"Now what would you like to wish for?" Ella waved her claws around as if conjuring magic.

"Um, me wish you get into lasagna so us eat you," Dumbdalf answered.

"Really? I can grant you a wish . . . *any* wish, and all you can come up with is to make me into lasagna?!" Ella was feeling more courageous. "Come on! I can grant you any wish you want! You guys've gotta think BIGGER!"

"Okay! Okay! Me got good one!" Dumberdoor said excitedly and smiled to Dumbdalf. "You ready? It totally best wish! Me wish that Sparkly Sparkle Glitter Pop *and* Smelly McUgly get into lasagna so us eat you both!"

"Ooooh! That *is* good wish!" Dumbdalf gave Dumberdoor a high five. "Me wish me thought of that one!"

"*Fine.* We'll both get into the lasagna so you can eat us," Ella proclaimed with a sigh. "But! Before we grant your wish, you must complete a challenge!"

"Is challenge to eat you?" Dumbdalf asked.

"No, you've gotta find . . . a talking platypus!" Ella said.

"A talking *pink* platypus!" Owen added to his sister's plan, hoping to make the task so impossible that the trolls would never be able to do it.

"Named Platyplat-plat-plat!" Ella said, trying to not giggle.

"And he has to play the ukulele!" Owen said, doing his best to not laugh.

"Upside down," Ella finished.

The two trolls scratched their heads, confused.

"Me gotta find talking pink what-a-pus named Platyplat-plat-plat...." Dumberdoor began.

"And he gotta play uke-something, uh, upside down?" Dumbdalf added.

"You got it! Now get to it!" Ella cheered.

The none-too-bright trolls rushed off into Terror Swamp on their impossible mission.

"We'll never see those two again!" Ella excitedly flapped her wings faster.

"How come I've always gotta be the smelly and ugly one?!" Owen complained as he tore off his disguise.

"You know what they say: 'If the wings fit . . .'" Ella pulled off her disguise and used her claws to slash the ropes that held the knights.

"I . . . I don't understand. Why are you saving us?" a confused Barry asked.

"Because we want to show you that not all dragons are bad," Ella answered.

"Is *that* why we're doing this?!" A surprised Owen smacked the ground with his tail. "I thought we were doing this so they'd give us some stinky fish strudel!"

"And to get some stinky fish strudel," Ella added, wrinkling her snout.

"Thanks for helping us and showing us the error of our ways," Dragon Stomper said. "We'll never crush dragons again."

"There go all the best holidays," Dragon Crusher whined.

"Instead of using holidays as an excuse to attack fake dragons, why don't you use them as a time to really help others?" Owen asked.

"Oh yeah. That sounds *so much* more fun than bashing the straw out of dragons," Dragon Crusher said sarcastically.

"Is it too late to put them into the lasagna?" Owen asked Ella.

9

ALL'S WELL THAT ENDS WITH NO ONE GETTING EATEN

Ella, Owen, and the four knights returned to the castle and were greeted with cheers of "Hurray! Hurray! The knights of Camelnot have captured whatever those things are!" by the villagers.

"No! No! No! We didn't capture them!"
Dragon Crusher quickly corrected.
"They're our friends!"

"They're dragons," Dragon Thumper
explained.

This shocking news was met by a chorus of cheers. "Hurray! Hurray! The knights of Camelnot made friends with evil dragons!"

"No! No! No! They're nice!" Dragon Stomper quickly corrected. "Not all dragons are evil!"

"Not evil?!" a villager named Byron said with a scoff. "Next you're gonna try to tell us that they're not made of straw!"

"We're not!" Ella finally spoke up.

"Then what are you made of?!" Byron laughed. "*Dragon?!*"

"It doesn't matter what they're made of," Dragon Stomper added. "What does matter is that we've been wrong about them this whole time and we need to treat them as equals!"

"*Equals?!*" a villager named Gwendolyn gasped. "There go all the best holidays!"

The bard held up his mandolin. "What am I supposed to do with this if I can't bash straw dragons with it?"

"You could try playing *music* with it," Owen said.

"You can play *music* on these things?!" the shocked bard asked. "*Really?*"

"And now, to give thanks for all that Ella and Owen have done for us, we knights of Camelnot have taken new names!" Barry announced.

"From henceforth, I shall be called Sir Dragon Buddy!" Dragon Crusher called out.

"And *I* want to be known as Sir Dragon Pal," Dragon Stomper proclaimed with a cheer.

"And *I* will be Sir Dragon Don't-Quite-Love-Them-Yet-But-Don't-Exactly-Hate-Them-Anymore," Dragon Thumper said.

Barry proclaimed, "And from this day forward, I shall be forever known as . . . Carl."

The knights and villagers of Camelnot bowed deeply as Ella and Owen waved good-bye—but not before Owen made sure to get the stinkiest fish strudel in the castle.

"I'm waiting. . . ." Ella said as they flew down the path.

"You're right, sis," Owen said. "This was all *your* fault."

"I meant that I'm waiting for you to admit that my plans are better than yours," Ella replied.

"Nope," Owen said.

"Yep," Ella replied.

"Nopey-nope-nope-nope-nope."

"Yeppy-yep-yep-yep-yep."

THUD! THUD! THUD!

The two trolls from Terror Swamp suddenly rushed out of the forest toward them. Ella and Owen skidded to a stop in midair.

"We got 'um! We got 'um!" Dumbdalf shouted. "Hey! What happened to all your moss?"

"We, uh, wished it away!" Ella explained, as they no longer had their troll fairy disguises.

Owen was the first to realize this could only mean more trouble for him. And probably Ella, too. The two dim-witted trolls had somehow found a platypus. A *pink* platypus carrying a ukulele to be exact, which he played . . . upside down. Somehow.

Owen gulped. "Oh, no. Please don't tell me your name is—"

The pink platypus cut off Owen and sang, "*You got it. My name is Platyplat-plat-plat and I love to siiiiiiiing!*"

"Me did what you said!" Dumberdoor said with a snarl. "Now me want us wishes!"

"And me wish you get in the lasagna!"

Dumbdalf added, thrusting the cauldron of lasagna before Ella and Owen.

Ella and Owen exchanged a worried look.

"Got any more bright ideas?" Owen whispered to Ella.

Unfortunately, Ella didn't have any ideas at all this time!

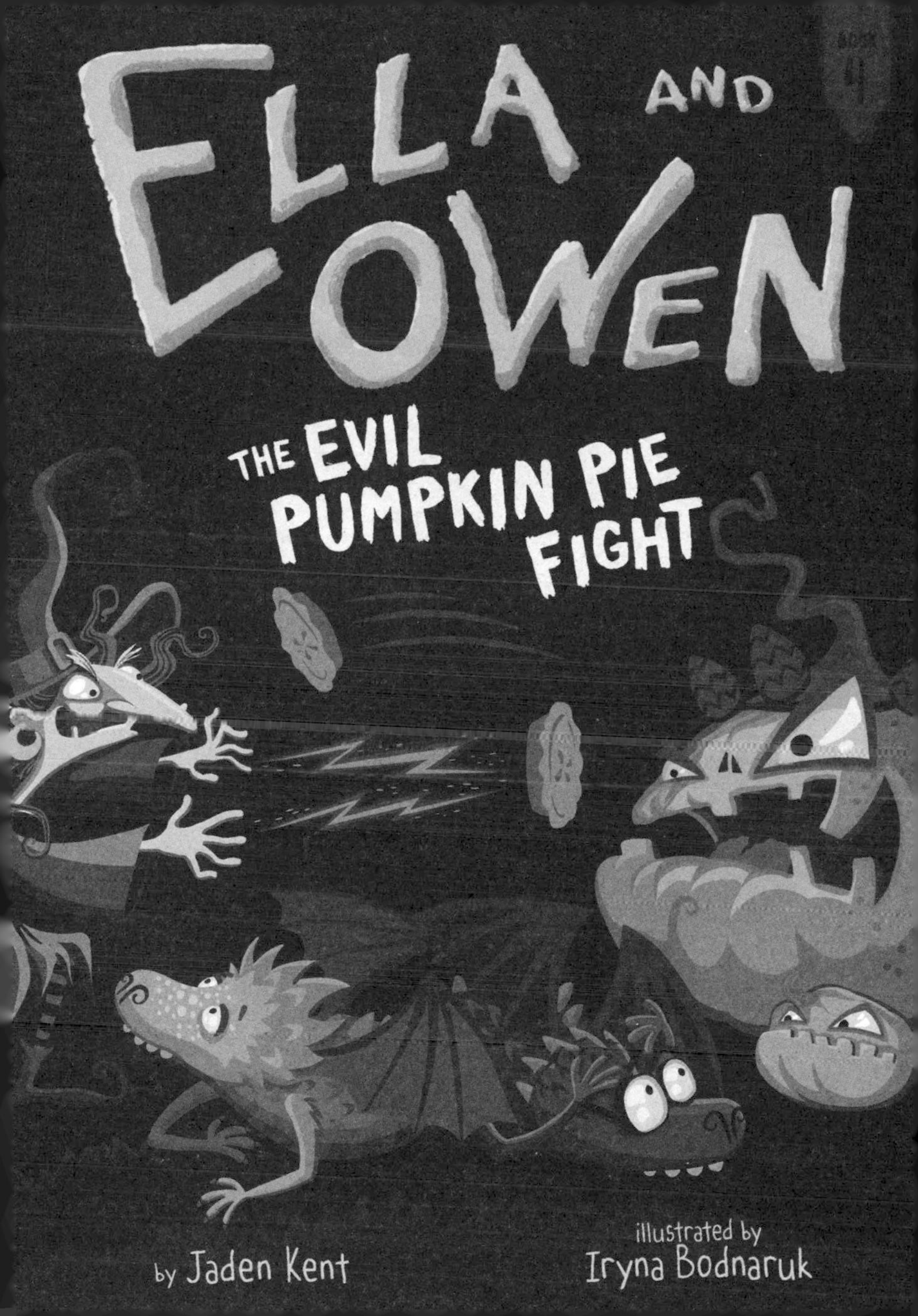
ELLA AND OWEN
THE EVIL PUMPKIN PIE FIGHT
by Jaden Kent
illustrated by
Iryna Bodnaruk

TABLE OF CONTENTS

"Give us me wishes!" Dumberdoor the troll said.

"We found the pink platypus that plays the ukulele upside down!" Dumbdalf, the other troll, said. "Now you owe us wishes."

The two trolls raced out from the forest toward Ella and Owen.

The dragon twins were shocked.

"How did they find a pink platypus?" Owen asked his sister.

"I don't even want to know about the ukulele," she replied.

"So, where's me wishes?" Dumberdoor demanded.

"Okay, okay. I have your first wish," Owen said. The trolls rubbed their hairy, wart-covered hands together with excitement.

"Your first wish is that you wish you could watch me and Ella run away!" Owen and Ella turned and ran away.

"Me not want that wish!" Dumberdoor said. "Me wish for dragon stew!"

"Me, too, wish for stew dragon!" Dumbdalf added. "Grant me wish!"

The trolls watched as the two dragons ran into the forest and disappeared into the shadows.

"I think we lost them," Ella said.

"I hope so," Owen puffed. "My claws are aching from all that running and my wings are too tired to flutter."

Owen looked around. "Wait a minute! We're back in Terror Swamp again! I didn't want that either!"

"Don't worry. I think home is this way," Ella said, pointing through the trees, ". . . or maybe it's that way."

"Good," Owen replied. "You go that way. I'm going the other way." Owen ran away but crashed into a tree. A branch broke off and fell on his head. "It's a Swamp Tree Goblin! It's got me!" Owen's scaly body wobbled and he tripped over a tree stump. He crashed into Ella.

"Watch where you're going!" she cried.

Ella and Owen splashed down into the inky black doom of Terror Swamp.

Ella shivered, shaking the water from her scales. "Don't be such a scaredy-dragon," she said. "There's hardly any water here."

Owen stood up and picked the mud off of his claws. "Great. So we're lost again."

"Maybe not," she replied. Ella pointed toward something moving on the other side of some trees. There was a flickering light in the distance. "Let's check that out," she said.

"Oh, let's not," Owen replied. "Every time we go check out something, we get captured and something tries to eat us."

"It could be a way out of Terror Swamp," she said.

"Really?!" Owen said. "There's no way I'm going to investigate the *only* light glowing in the middle of a place called Terror Swamp!" Owen folded his scaly arms. He wasn't budging.

"Well, I'm going to go see what it is. You can stay here. On your own. In the dark." Ella's dragon wings fluttered and she flew off toward the light.

Owen looked around as it grew darker. Leaves rustled and swirled in the night air.

A Grizzly Owl hooted.

A Swamp Bat swooped low, passing by Owen's snout.

On second thought, being left all alone while someone else goes to check out the only light glowing in the middle of a place called Terror Swamp is even worse than going to check out the only light glowing in the middle of a place called Terror Swamp! Owen thought.

Owen flew off after his sister. "Okay, Ella! Wait up! Let's see what's making that light!"

Together, the two dragons pushed through the forest. They came to a clearing in front of a broken-down wooden swamp shack. A jack-o'-lantern with an angry face carved into it sat on the porch. Light flickered from the candle inside of it.

"That's one creepy jack-o'-lantern!" Ella said.

"Okay, we've seen what the light is. Let's leave," Owen said. "This place looks haunted."

"You can't ever go," the jack-o'-lantern suddenly said to them. "Ever-never!"

"Who-who are you?" Ella stuttered.

"I am . . . the Pumpkin King!" he said. "Vines up!"

"AHHHHHHHH!" Ella and Owen screamed.

Vines stretched out from beneath the porch and wrapped around Ella and Owen.

"I told you something like this would happen!" Owen yelled.

"**J**ust what are you the king of?" Ella asked. The Pumpkin King's head sat on the wooden floor inside the swamp shack. The dragon siblings sat on the floor, wrapped tightly in leafy green vines.

"Right now, I'm the king of, well . . . just this shack," the Pumpkin King replied. "But I have very big plans for next year! Soon

I'll be king of those rocks over there and maybe those bushes right outside the front door."

"It's good to have dreams," Owen said. "Can you let us go now?"

"Never!" the Pumpkin King said. "You're working for the witch! She already stole my body, and now you're here to steal my royal crown!"

Ella and Owen saw the king's "crown" resting on a broken chair. The crown was made of twigs and pinecones. A beetle crawled lazily across it.

"Looks . . . um . . . fantastic," Ella said.

Owen snorted, and Ella elbowed him to keep him from laughing.

"You try making a crown without any arms and see how well you do!" the Pumpkin King huffed.

"We don't work for anyone!" Ella said.

"And we don't know any witches either," said Owen.

"We're just lost," Ella explained.

"We want out of Terror Swamp and we want to go home!" Owen explained.

"If you're not spies, maybe we can make a deal," the Pumpkin King said.

"What kind of deal?" asked Ella.

"A royal deal! I'll give you a map that will take you out of Terror Swamp," the Pumpkin King said.

TERRIBLE WITCH LIVES HERE

CREEPY GRAVEYARD

WAY OUT

TERROR SWAMP

"That's great!" Owen said.

"And in return, you have to go GET MY BODY BACK FROM THAT WITCH!"

"Why can't you just go get your body back yourself?" Ella asked.

"I've been growing a pumpkin army to attack that witch and steal back my body, but it's taking way too long," the Pumpkin King explained. "Did you know that pumpkins take months to grow? And pumpkin kings are terrible farmers. Also, I've got this itch that's killing me. And don't even ask me about how hard it is to make pies without a body!"

"Uh, pies?" Owen asked.

"Yes! Pies!" the Pumpkin King snapped, tilting his head to motion to the stacks and stacks of pies in the corner of his shack.

"That's a LOT of pies," Ella gasped.

"Eleventy-raccoon at last count!" the Pumpkin King proudly announced.

"Uh, 'eleventy-raccoon' isn't a number," Ella said.

"Whattya expect?! My head's *hollow*, okay?!" the Pumpkin King griped. "Also, math wasn't required at Pumpkin King School."

"Okay, we'll help you," Ella agreed.

"Wait! We'll do *what*?" Owen exclaimed.

"In exchange for the map," Ella added.

"Can you throw in something to eat, too? A little fire thorn stew?" Owen suggested. "Fish bone casserole? Screamer Beetle nachos with extra screams?"

"All I have are pumpkin seeds," the Pumpkin King replied.

"We'll still do it," Ella said. She grabbed a handful of seeds that were scattered around the shack and popped them into her mouth. Then she grabbed another handful for later.

"So this witch . . ." Owen began. "I'll bet she lives on the other side of a creepy graveyard?"

"No," the Pumpkin King corrected.

"Whew! That's a relief!" Owen replied.

"She lives in the *middle* of a creepy graveyard," the Pumpkin King finished.

"Great," Owen said with a groan.

"It's quiet," Owen whispered. "Too quiet."

"Shhhhh!" Ella whispered back. "It's not quiet if you keep talking."

Ella and Owen tiptoed through the dark graveyard. Headstones stuck out from the mossy ground. Leafy vines

hung from trees and wrapped around their trunks. Owls hooted. Bats flew overhead. Wind rattled the iron gates of the cemetery. A thick fog covered the ground.

"Watch your step, Ella," Owen said. "I can't see my claws in the fog and—oof!" Owen tripped over a headstone and fell to the ground. **"OUCH!"**

"Shhhh!"

"No one can hear us in a graveyard," Owen said.

"I know. I just hate graveyards," Ella whispered. "They remind me of cemeteries."

"Graveyards and cemeteries are the same thing," Owen said.

"That explains it, then," Ella whispered back.

"Don't tell me you're suddenly afraid," Owen said. "One of us has to be a brave dragon."

"I'm not afraid of the dark," she replied. "I'm not afraid of bats, rats, vampires, or even witches." She paused and took a deep breath. "But I am afraid of zombies."

"Zombies? They're already dead. You can't be afraid of dead things."

"They eat dragon brains," Ella said. "And I'd prefer my brain to stay in my head."

"Okay then, since you want out of here faster, you go first," Owen said.

"Well, since you're not scared of zombies, *you* go first," Ella said, nudging Owen forward.

"Since you're more scared than I am, you go first more," Owen said. He pushed Ella to take the lead.

"Who dares disturb my slumber?" A ghostly specter rose up from the ground.

"Okay! Now I'm scared!" Owen gasped.

"I'm scared more!" Ella said.

"Not as much as I am!" Owen said.

"Like ten bajillion times more than you!" Ella replied.

"Um, excuse me," the ghost said. "Remember me? Angry ghost? In the cemetery?"

"Be with you in a sec, Mr. Ghost," Owen said then turned back to Ella. "Well, *I'm* waaaay more scared than if I woke up and found a thousand headless Screamer Scorpions crawling under my pillow!"

"Uh, guys?" the ghost interrupted.

They both ignored the ghost and continued to argue over who was more scared.

"And *I'm* even more scared than if I woke up and found out that I looked like *you*!" Ella said to Owen.

"WOOOOO-HOOOOOOO!"

the ghost howled. Ella's and Owen's wings shivered. The ghostly voice had stopped Ella and Owen from arguing. They flew backward in a panic . . . and landed in a huge spiderweb.

"Okay, now I'm really scared," Owen said. He tried to pull himself out of the web. "And we're stuck, too."

"I'd love to help," the ghost said, "but I really don't like spiders." He sunk back into the ground and disappeared.

"Don't move," Owen said to Ella.

"Why?" she asked.

"Unless I'm mistaken, this is the web of a giant twelve-fanged Vampire Tree Spider," he said. "I've seen pictures of them in a book called *Spiders That Can Eat a Dragon*. Oh no! It's seen us!"

The giant twelve-fanged Vampire Tree Spider slid out from a web tunnel at the top of the tree. It slowly and hungrily creeped toward Ella and Owen.

"Did you ever notice that a lot of things want to eat us lately?" Ella asked. She tugged on the web and kicked as hard as she could. She was stuck, too.

"Of course they do," Owen replied. "*I'm very tasty.*"

The spider moved closer. Its eight hairy legs skated across the web.

"Tasty! That's it! Ella, do you still have those seeds from the Pumpkin King?"

"Food? You're thinking about food when we're about to *be* food?!" Ella yelled.

"Let's give the spider something that isn't dragon meat!" Owen cried.

The spider crept right up to the trapped dragons. Drool dripped from its hungry mouth. It was close enough for Owen to count ten of its twelve fangs.

The spider jumped at Ella, eager for a yummy dragon snack. Ella ducked and threw her extra pumpkin seeds into the spider's mouth.

The spider happily gobbled them down and burped. No longer hungry, it crawled to the edge of its web and lay down to sleep. It would not be eating two dragons . . . yet.

"Nice job, Ella!" Owen yelled. He finally managed to hook one of his thumb claws into the web and cut them free.

The two dragons plopped to the ground and took off.

WARTS UP?

"**O**kay, now *that* looks spooky," Owen said. "I told you we shouldn't have come here."

The witch's home sat in the middle of the cemetery, just like the Pumpkin King had said. The cottage was quiet and still. Moss covered much of the roof, and many of the windows were dark. But a light in one window suggested someone was inside.

"How are we supposed to sneak in and get the Pumpkin King's body back from the witch?" Owen asked.

"I have an idea," Ella said. She grabbed some mud and slapped it onto Owen's face, covering him with moss and swamp muck.

"Ow, I'm going to get scale warts!" Owen complained.

"Quiet, please," Ella said. "I'm making you into something witches love: a zombie."

The mud covered Owen's entire face. "Yuck!" he said. Ella stuck a couple of twigs and leaves onto Owen's muddy face. "But you're scared of zombies."

"I am. But I've heard that witches love zombies," she said. Then she slapped mud onto her own face and spread it all around, covering her long snout.

"Now we just walk and talk like two mindless zombies," Ella explained. "Then we can knock on the witch's door and she'll let us in." She smiled. "And that's when we take back the Pumpkin King's body."

Ella and Owen stumbled in the direction of the witch's house. Owen held one leg stiff and dragged it along the ground. Ella stretched out her arms in front of her body.

"Braaaaains," Ella groaned. "Must . . . have . . . braaaains!"

"Chocolate caaaaake," Owen groaned. Ella glared at him. "What?! I don't wanna eat brains! They're gross!"

They lumbered up to the front door of the cottage. Ella banged on the door with her foot.

The door opened slightly. The witch peered out from behind it.

"Braaaaains," Ella groaned.

"Oh, zombies! I haven't had zombie guests for weeks!" the witch said. "What can I do for you delightful walking undead?"

"Braaaaains," Ella groaned again.

The witch nodded and turned to Owen, waiting for his answer.

"Ummmm . . . soup?" Owen groaned.

"What kind of zombie eats *soup*?" the witch asked.

"Don't mind him," Ella groaned. "He stopped making sense after I ate his . . . braaaaains."

The witch opened the door all the way. Ella and Owen stumbled inside. "Where are you zombies from anyway?"

"Zombie . . . ville?" Owen replied, not quite sure where zombies would come from.

"Zombieville? I've never heard of Zombieville," the witch replied.

"It's across the Zombie Bridge from Zombieburg," Ella added. "It's a very small village."

"Let's have lunch," the witch said. "I'm all out of brains and soup, but I do have a nice stew in my cauldron." She dipped a ladle into the pot and pulled out an oddly shaped object.

"AAAAAAAAH! BRAINS!" Owen screamed and jumped into Ella's arms.

"It's not a brain! It's a *turnip*!" Ella said.

"AAAAAAAAH! TURNIPS!" Owen screamed. He jumped from Ella's grasp and into the witch's arms.

The witch fell over backward from his weight. Owen landed on top of her. **"OOF,"** she oofed.

"You're *not* really zombies!" the witch said.

"**A**w, dragon scales! How'd you know that we weren't zombies?" Ella asked, shocked. "Did you cast some powerful magic spell?"

"Didn't need to. Even the worst zombie knows the difference between a turnip and a brain. And the last time I checked, zombies don't have *tails*." The witch pointed to Ella's and Owen's tails sticking out from under their disguises.

"Oops," Ella said. Her green cheeks turned red with embarrassment. "I'm Ella and this is my brother, Owen."

"My name is Rainbow Sparkles," the witch said. "Why did you come to my cottage?"

"I thought witches were named stuff like Warty Wart Hag Face and Hairy Wart Hag Face and Warty Hairy Warty Wart . . . Hag Face," Owen said.

"You read too many books, kid," Rainbow Sparkles replied. "Now tell me why you're here or I'll turn you into puppies!"

"NOOOOOOO! Not that! Wait . . . *puppies*?" Owen said.

"Yeah. *All* the other witches turn people into toads and newts. BOR-ING! It is *so* hard to find a witch with any imagination!" Rainbow Sparkles complained, then proudly added, "I'm the only one doing cute puppies."

"Tell her why we're here," Owen whispered to Ella.

"And get turned into a puppy? No way!" Ella whispered back.

"Okay, I'll do it," Owen said. "But just think about how mad Mom and Dad will be when they find out you let some witch named Raincloud Popsicle or whatever turn me into a little dog."

"Dragon drool! I'd rather be a puppy!" Ella said and faced Rainbow Sparkles. "The Pumpkin King sent us here to get his body back. He said you, um, kinda . . . uh . . . sorta . . . stole it?"

Ella closed her eyes, folded her wings into her back, and got ready to be turned into a puppy.

"Don't worry, Sis. I promise to take you for a walk every day once you're a puppy," Owen whispered to Ella.

"Or probably every *other* day."

"That's a lie!" Rainbow Sparkles huffed. "I never stole anybody . . . or any *body*! The Pumpkin King's body came to live with me because its pumpkin head was grumpy and mean! The pumpkin head was always forcing his body to make pies. Pies, pies, and pies! Nothing but pies!"

"What's wrong with pies?" Ella asked, slowly opening her eyes.

"Nothing. But it'd be nice if he was allowed to bake a cake now and then! You know, just to mix things up," Rainbow Sparkles said.

"I have a question," Owen said.

"Yes?" Rainbow Sparkles replied.

"Are you gonna turn my sister into a puppy or what?" Owen asked. "'Cause I wanna name her Ruff-Ruff Doggy-Doggy Bark Face!"

Before Rainbow Sparkles could reply, the Pumpkin King's headless body, which was stuffed with straw like a scarecrow, stumbled into the room. Without its pumpkin head, the body couldn't see where it was walking and it bonked into the table, then a wall, then it walked into a closet before finding its way over to Rainbow Sparkles.

"The Pumpkin King's body wants to live with me because . . ." Rainbow Sparkles giggled and hugged the headless straw body. "We're in love!"

"You know what, Owen? This just got _really_ weird," Ella said.

6

PUMPKIN PIE PANDEMONIUM

"**W**e've got good news and bad news, o' King," Ella said to the Pumpkin King after they returned to his shack. Her tail nervously wagged behind her. "The bad news is . . . your body's not coming back. But the good news is . . . you're invited to a wedding!"

The Pumpkin King's orange head turned
red with anger! "NOT COMING BACK?!"
he shouted. Pumpkin seeds shot from his
mouth. "Grab all the pumpkin pies you can
carry and follow me!"

The Pumpkin King hopped out to his garden and commanded, "Pumpkin army! Time to battle the witch!"

"But we're not fully grown yet, your royal orangeness," one of the softball-sized pumpkins said in a squeaky voice. "But we are cuuuuuute."

"Um, like, maybe if you could come back in a month or so, we'd be, like, totally big?" a second pumpkin squeaked.

"I can't wait a month! If you're big enough to carry a pie, you're big enough to fight a witch!" the Pumpkin King responded as he bounced away from the swamp shack.

"Can't argue with that logic," Owen said to Ella.

Dozens of small pumpkins broke from their vines. Some were round and some were oblong. Some had lumps while others had bumps. They hopped along after the Pumpkin King like a mess of orange bouncing balls.

Ella and Owen fluttered along after the pumpkins, doing their best to carry the teetering towers of pumpkin pies they held in their clawed hands.

"Why are we helping him?" Owen asked. "He's kinda nuts."

"He's not kinda nuts. He's *completely* nuts," Ella replied. "But we've gotta get the Pumpkin King's map so we can get out of Terror Swamp. Just play along until we think of a plan."

Once they reached Rainbow Sparkles's cottage, the Pumpkin King ordered Owen and Ella to place a pie atop each of his pumpkin soldiers' heads.

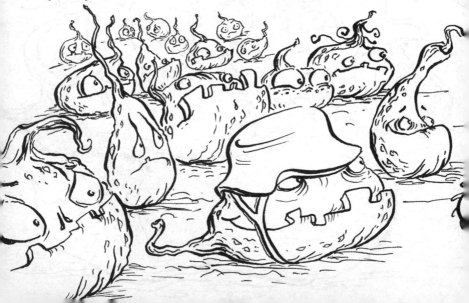

"Are you gonna invite the witch to a picnic?" Owen asked.

"Yes. A picnic of doooooooom!" The Pumpkin King laughed.

"Maybe it'd be better if you just made her a sandwich?" Ella said.

"I'm in charge of the picnic—I mean battle—not you!" the Pumpkin King answered. "Launch the sandwiches—I mean pies—my pumpkin army!"

The pumpkins hopped off the ground
and launched the pumpkin pies from their
heads.

The pies hit Rainbow Sparkles's cottage
and splattered ooey, gooey pumpkin pie
filling everywhere, covering the entire
building.

"I'll get you for that, you grumpy ol' pumpkin head!" Rainbow Sparkles shouted as she ran from her cottage with the Pumpkin King's body beside her. She waved her wand and conjured up her own swarm of floating apple pies, which she then sent flying toward the Pumpkin King and his army.

Ella dove to her left to avoid being hit, but Owen wasn't fast enough and an apple pie hit him square in the snout.

SPLAT!

"This is the tastiest battle I've ever seen!" he said merrily, licking the pie from his face. "I hope someone starts throwing some creamy worm pies, too!"

Each side threw pie after pie at the other as chaos broke out. Rainbow Sparkles conjured up more pies out of thin air and threw them at the pumpkin army. Even the Pumpkin King's body was throwing pies but, as it didn't have eyes, only managed to throw them into some bushes.

"I know how we can stop this pie fight!" Ella said, dodging an apple pie.

"With an army of annoyed bananas?" Owen said.

"No! With a spider!" Ella replied and grabbed two pies. "Follow me!"

"Snails and tails! I'd rather try our luck with a whole mess of annoyed bananas." Owen sighed but followed his sister anyway.

"**L**ast chance to go find some annoyed bananas," Owen said as they ran back to the spiderweb that had held them earlier. "Or how about a grumpy papaya?"

"Nope. We stick with the plan," Ella replied.

"Is part of the plan getting eaten by a giant spider?" a nervous Owen asked.

"Of course not," Ella said.

"Then we better start flying!" Owen shouted.

"HISSSSS!" the Vampire Tree Spider hissed as it spied the approaching dragons.

The huge spider jumped up and tried to pluck Owen and Ella out of the air and into its slobbery mandibles.

"Dragon wings, don't fail me now!" Owen said and quickly zoomed away.

Ella followed him, crushing up the pies in her hands and leaving a trail of pie crumbs behind her.

The spider happily gobbled up the bits of pie as it chased the two dragons.

Ella and Owen flapped their wings as quickly as they could and barely stayed ahead of the scampering spider just below them.

When they got back to Rainbow Sparkles's cottage, both sides were still throwing pies at each other, but now Rainbow Sparkles was conjuring up doughnuts as well. The Pumpkin King's pumpkin army was covered in pie filling, frosting, and doughnut sprinkles.

"This battle is worse than getting ice beetles stuck in your scales!" Ella said.

"I know! And it's a total waste of dessert, too!" Owen added gloomily.

But the appearance of the giant spider put an instant end to the battle. The spider spun a huge web, trapping Ella, Owen, the Pumpkin King, the pumpkin army, Rainbow Sparkles, and the Pumpkin King's body within it like flies.

"Hey! One of your crazy plans worked again, Sis!" Owen said. "But now how're we gonna stop the giant spider from eating us?"

"I kinda, sorta, didn't think about that part," Ella confessed.

The spider crept closer to Ella and Owen. Spider drool dripped onto Ella's wings.

"Wing warts! I hate spider drool!" Ella said.

"You'd better hope spiders like chocolate doughnuts or we're gonna be dragon-shaped spider snacks!" Owen flapped his wings as hard as he could and, despite being stuck in the web, managed to create a small breeze that blew a pile of doughnuts toward the spider. The spider sniffed them once, twice, then happily gobbled them up.

But the Pumpkin King was even angrier than before. "Get me out of this web!" he shouted.

"Don't worry. I saved a jelly-filled one for you," Owen assured him.

"I don't want a doughnut!" the Pumpkin King snarled, spitting pumpkin seeds from his mouth. "I. Want. My. BODY!"

"Your body wants to stay with Rainbow Sparkles," Ella explained.

"That's impossible!" the Pumpkin King huffed. "That witch cast a spell on my body. That's the only way it would want to stay with her."

"I did no such thing!" Rainbow Sparkles protested.

Despite the webbing that held them like glue, Rainbow Sparkles and the Pumpkin King's body managed to reach out and hug each other.

"We're in love!" Rainbow Sparkles giggled.

"Okay. This just got *really* weird," the Pumpkin King said.

Even a grouchy old thing like the Pumpkin King knew no pumpkin army could ever defeat the power of love, so he agreed that his body could marry Rainbow Sparkles. Luckily the spider liked chocolate doughnuts more than dragons, pumpkins, and witches, so it freed everyone from its web . . . as long as they kept feeding it doughnuts.

All the ghouls, banshees, ghosts, and goblins in Terror Swamp were invited to the wedding of Rainbow Sparkles and the Pumpkin King's body. Some zombies even lumbered over all the way from Zombie Town to join in the festivities.

Ella and Owen sat in the front row next to the now-less-grumpy-but-still-a-little-grumpy Pumpkin King, who wore a fancy top hat. The pumpkin army, dressed in matching tuxedoes, sang songs as Rainbow Sparkles, dressed in a wedding gown made of cobwebs, walked down the aisle with dead, black flowers hanging from a broomstick.

"Braaaaains . . ." a zombie in a ripped and dirty dress sitting next to Owen said.

"Sorry. Dinner's not until after the ceremony," Owen replied.

The ghostly specter from the graveyard floated over to the front of the gathering. "Dearly beloved . . . and dearly deceased, cursed, headless, haunted, and undead," he groaned loudly. "We are gathered here today to celebrate the wedding of Rainbow Sparkles the witch and the Pumpkin King's body, who wishes to be called Headless Joe."

"Bwaaaaaaaa!" the Pumpkin King blubbered. "I always cry at weddings. Especially when it's my body getting married."

Ella gently wiped away the Pumpkin King's tears. "We don't want you getting all moldy before they cut the wedding cake," she said.

Rainbow Sparkles and Headless Joe exchanged their rings, although Headless Joe, being unable to see because he had no head, stuck Rainbow Sparkles's ring on the end of her pointed nose.

"I now pronounce you witch and headless-body-stuffed-with-straw!" the ghostly specter announced with a groan.

Rainbow Sparkles and Headless Joe walked back down the aisle as their guests threw handfuls of beetles at them.

"This is easily the strangest wedding I've ever been to," Ella whispered to her brother.

"I know!" Owen agreed. "I can't wait to see how they celebrate birthdays!"

The wedding was over and the guests had all floated or lumbered home . . . or crawled back into the nearest grave.

"I can't thank you enough!" Rainbow Sparkles said to Ella and Owen. "None of this would've happened without your help."

"You know, if a kooky witch and a dude named Headless Joe can't find love in the nightmarish Terror Swamp, what hope do the rest of us have?" Owen said.

"You dragons kept your part of our deal," the Pumpkin King said. "It's not your fault my body wants someone else." He handed Owen a map that would lead them out of Terror Swamp.

"Thanks, Pumpkin King!" Owen replied.

"So, no more pie fights for you?" Ella asked.

"No. I never knew my pumpkin army was so talented until I heard them sing at the ceremony," the Pumpkin King explained. "So we're starting a singing group!"

"LAAAAAAAAAAA!" the former pumpkin army sang in unison.

"We call ourselves the Smashing Pumpkins Pie," the Pumpkin King said proudly.

"Before we go, Owen and I want to give you guys some gifts, too," Ella said.

Ella put her fingers to her mouth, gave a loud whistle, and the giant Vampire Tree Spider drifted down from overhead, still eating chocolate doughnuts.

"We had the spider make you a new body!" Owen said to the Pumpkin King.

The spider held out a fancy new body woven from spider silk. Ella gently lifted the Pumpkin King and placed him atop the silky body.

"Thank you! It is so nice to have hands again!" The Pumpkin King scratched an itchy spot on the back of his lumpy head.

Owen handed Rainbow Sparkles a book. "And here's something for you and Headless Joe."

"A cake cookbook! I love it!" Rainbow Sparkles said. "Dear! Look what Ella and Owen got us!"

Rainbow Sparkles showed the cookbook to Headless Joe . . . who promptly walked into a tree.

"I'll just show it to him later," Rainbow Sparkles said.

With everyone happy, Owen and Ella said their final goodbyes and set off toward home. But little did they know that the two trolls, Dumberdoor and Dumbdalf, had not given up on their search for Ella and Owen and were in fact hiding behind some trees just down the trail from where the dragons were.

"Get the stew pot ready! Here come them two now!" Dumberdoor said.

"Us is gonna have a yummy dragon dinner tonight!" Dumbdalf replied as Ella and Owen made their way ever closer to the two hidden trolls. . . .

JADEN KENT is a dynamic author duo. They are Emmy Award—winning writers for children's TV shows, as well as the authors of numerous children's chapter books.

IRYNA BODNARUK is a Ukrainian children's illustrator currently living in Cyprus. Visit her online at keep-fun.com.

LOOK FOR
MORE BOOKS IN THE
ELLA AND OWEN
SERIES!

#5 THE GREAT TROLL QUEST

#6 DRAGON SPIES

#7 TWIN TROUBLE

#8 THE WORST PET

#9 GRUMPY GOBLINS

#10 THE DRAGON GAMES

DISCOVER YOUR NEXT FAVORITE SERIES

Tales of SASHA

Meet Sasha, one very special horse who discovers she can fly! With the help of her best friend, Wyatt, Sasha sets out to find other flying horses like her. Come along on their adventures as they explore new places and make new friends.

THE ALIEN NEXT DOOR

Harris thinks there's something strange about the new kid at school, Zeke, and that's because Zeke is the new kid on the planet! As Harris looks for the truth, Zeke realizes that he has a lot to learn about Earth and blending in. Will Zeke be able to make friends, or will Harris discover his secret? Join their adventures that are out of this world.

ALSO AVAILABLE AS 4 BOOKS IN 1!

Isle of MISFITS

Gibbon is a gargoyle who doesn't like to sit still. But a chance meeting brings him to an island filled with other mythical creatures and a special school for misfits like him! Gibbon and his new friends get all the excitement they can handle in this magical series!

Mighty MEG

Meg's life is turned upside down when a magical ring gives her superpowers! But Meg isn't the only one who changes. Strange things start happening in her once-normal town. Can Meg master her new powers and find the courage to be the hero her town needs?